Geronimo Stilton

LOST IN TIME

THE FOURTH JOURNEY THROUGH TIME

Scholastic Inc.

Published by Scholastic Inc., *Publishers since 1920*, 557 Broadway, New York, NY 10012. SCHOLASTIC and associated logos are trademarks and/or registered trademarks of Scholastic Inc.

Stilton is the name of a famous English cheese. It is a registered trademark of the Stilton Cheese Makers' Association. For more information, go to www.stiltoncheese.com.

ISBN 978-1-338-08877-9

Text by Geronimo Stilton
Original title *Viaggio nel Tempo - 4*
Cover by Silvia Bigolin (design and color)
Illustrations by Danilo Barozzi, Silvia Bigolin, and Danilo Loizedda (design); Christian Aliprandi (color); and Piemme's archives. 3-D backgrounds by Davide Turotti.
Graphics by Yuko Egusa

Special thanks to Beth Dunfey
Translated by Julia Heim
Interior design by Kay Petronio

10 9 8 7 6 5 4 3 2 1   17 18 19 20 21

Printed in China   62

First edition, February 2017

GERONIMO'S TRAVELS THROUGH TIME

Dear mouse friends, welcome to my latest journey through time! My pal Professor von Volt has taken us on some wild trips with his time-travel inventions . . .

MOUSE MOVER 3000

The Mouse Mover 3000 was the professor's first time machine. We used it to visit the dinosaurs of prehistoric times, ancient Egypt, and medieval Europe!

RODENT RELOCATOR

The Rodent Relocator was a more advanced time machine. On this adventure, we saw Caesar's Rome, discovered the secrets of Mayan cities, and even danced in the palace of Versailles during the time of the Sun King!

PAW PRO PORTAL

With the Paw Pro Portal, we reached the Ice Age, ancient Greece, and Renaissance Florence. We encountered some truly unforgettable rodents!

TAIL TRANSPORTER

This time, we traveled on board the Tail Transporter, which worked by dematerializing and rematerializing — a truly weird and unique experience! Squeak!

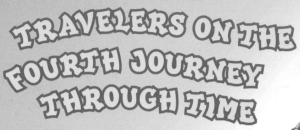

TRAVELERS ON THE FOURTH JOURNEY THROUGH TIME

Geronimo Stilton

Dear mouse friends, my name is Stilton, Geronimo Stilton, and I am about to tell you about a truly fabumouse adventure! But first things first: Let me introduce you to my friends!

Wild Willie

An archaeologist and lover of adventure, Wild Willie calls himself a "treasure hunter." He's very athletic, and his true passion is solving mysteries.

Maya

A fascinating rodent, Maya is Wild Willie's cousin and an archaeology student. She loves all extreme sports and absolutely adores adventure!

Benjamin Stilton

Benjamin is my favorite nephew! He is so kindhearted and sweet. And his dream is to become a great journalist, just like me!

Bugsy Wugsy

Bugsy is Benjamin's best friend. She's an adventurous and energetic rodent . . . a bit too enthusiastic at times! But I must admit, she has a heart of solid gold.

PAWS VON VOLT

A genius inventor, Professor von Volt is devoted to all kinds of science experiments. His latest invention is the Tail Transporter, the time-travel machine we used for this trip!

ROBORAT-8

A small robot created by Professor von Volt, he is the onboard computer for the Tail Transporter. He chatters constantly and can be a little cheeky . . . but he can solve almost any problem!

ACHOO! ACHOO! AAAAACHOOO!

It was a **freezing** winter afternoon. I was sitting in my pawchair, **wrapped** in three blankets, seven pairs of pajamas, three sweaters, two pairs of socks, slippers, a fuzzy hat with a pom-pom, fuzzy earmuffs, a tail cover, and even **wool** long underwear!

New Mouse City felt like the tip of Coldcreeps

Brrrr!

Peak. It was so chilly even a snowmouse would've put a coat on!

Despite the **cold** — and despite the fact that the mayor had told everyone to stay home — I tried to go out. It was my duty as a journalist.

You see, I am a very busy mouse. I run *The Rodent's Gazette,* the most famouse newspaper on Mouse Island. But by now I'm sure you've figured out who I am: My name is Stilton, *Geronimo Stilton*!

This is me, Geronimo Stilton!

Tuesday morning, I tried to get to the office, but the minute I stepped outside, I turned into an **ice cube**!

It took hours for me to thaw out again, and when I did, I discovered I'd caught the **WORST** cold of my life. That's why I was home in my pawchair, all **BUNDLED UP**, when the telephone rang. It was my aunt Sweetfur.

"Helwow? Who's dhere? Oh, hi, Aunt Sweetfur! What a nice surbrise!" I said, sneezing.

"Oh, my dear little Gerrykins, you sound terrible!" Aunt Sweetfur exclaimed. "You should take a steam bath with water from Brimstone Lake. It smells worse than rotten eggs, but it's an excellent remedy!"

It smells like rotten eggs!

"A STEAM BATH?"

"Yes, so you can breathe in the hot vapors. Just cover your snout with a towel . . ." She began listing a bunch of home remedies. I LISTENED for a few minutes, said thank you, and hung up.

The phone immediately rang again. It was my cousin Trap.

"Helwow? Who's dhere? Sdilton here, Geronibo Sdilton!"

5

It smells like
rotten fish!

"Cousin, what a nasty cold! You should take a hot bath with mud from the Sulfurous Swamp. It smells like **rotten fish**, but it works!"

"Bud from dhe Sulfurous Swamp?"

"No, you didn't understand: I said *mud*!"

"I bnow, that's whad I said: bud!"

"No, Cousin, I said *mud*!" Trap scolded me. "Try not to mess this up! If you get the **wrong** thing and the cure doesn't work, don't blame me!"

I thanked Trap and said that I understood — I just wasn't able to **pronounce** the name because of my cold.

I had just hung up when the phone **rang** again. This time it was my sister, Thea. "My dear Gerry Berry, how are you? Aunt Sweetfur told me that you have a really bad **cold**," she began. "You should drink some Mountain Mint Tea. The herb only grows on the cliffs of Stinko Peak, and it smells like **rancid rubbish**, but it's a surefire cure!"

I thanked Thea for her concern, but I assured her that I didn't need any **SUREFIRE** cure. Especially not one that smelled like **rotten** eggs, **rotten** fish, or **rotten** garbage! I'd just wait for the cold to pass naturally.

It smells like rancid rubbish!

The phone rang off the hook for the rest of the afternoon. I got calls from Tina Spicytail, who suggested I use hot compresses with stinkleaf that smelled like **rotten cabbage**, and Grandma Rose, who advised that I eat fresh algae, which is as slimy as a **GIANT SNAIL**.

It smells like rotten cabbage!

My last call came from my grandfather, William Shortpaws. He

As slimy as a giant snail!

didn't suggest any home remedies. Instead, he **SCOLDED** me. "Stop complaining, Grandson! Back in my day, I didn't let a LITTLE COLD get me down. I'd get to work even if I had to be driven in an ambulance and carried in on a stretcher!"

That was the conversation that made me realize I needed to take drastic action. I turned off my cell phone, unplugged the landline, unscrewed the doorbell, disconnected the intercom, and got into bed under a mountain of blankets.

You see, this was **MY** foolproof cure: curling up in my nice **warm** mouse hole and sleeping for three days in a row!

When I finally emerged from my burrow of blankets, I was completely healed. I looked out the window. The **sun** was shining, and even though it was winter, the streets of New Mouse City were crowded with rodents.

The cold front had passed!

I listened to my voice mail.

There were thirty phone calls from relatives and friends sharing their **surefire cures** for colds.

There were fifteen calls from Grandfather William, reminding me that he was a *real* editor with a true sense of duty, while I was weaker than a gooey strand of string cheese.

Finally, there were three messages from my old friend **Professor Paws von Volt** . . .

? ? ?
THREE MYSTERIOUS MESSAGES

In the **FIRST MESSAGE**, Professor von Volt asked about my health and requested that I call him as soon as possible. The tone of his squeak was a bit **agitated**.

PROFESSOR PAWS VON VOLT

The professor is a dear friend and an extraordinary inventor. He is also often in danger — no-good rodents are always trying to steal his inventions! His projects could become very dangerous in the wrong paws. As a result, the professor is so obsessed with secrecy — which usually makes it hard to locate him. I'm the only one who knows how to get ahold of him. We have our own supersecret system of communication: the Voltophone! I also have an emergency plan to find him, in case the professor is ever in peril.

In the **SECOND MESSAGE**, which the professor left just an hour later, he sounded even **more agitated**: "My dear Geronimo, our mutual friend Professor Cyril B. Sandsnout is in urgent need of help. I beg of you, call me back right away!" **Click!**

Worried, I listened to the **THIRD AND FINAL MESSAGE**. The professor's squeak now sounded **super-agitated**: "Dear Geronimo, I haven't heard back from you, which makes me think you must have a serious problem as well. But I must find a **SOLUTION** right away . . . I'll figure it out by myself!" **Click!**

Figure it out by himself? Holey cheese, Professor von Volt was too old to be going on **ADVENTURES**, especially by himself!

I called the professor immediately to apologize and explain that I'd been **SICK** in bed. But no one answered — not at home or on his cell.

At that point, I had only one option: I had to use the **VOLTOPHONE**, the **supersecret** communicati on system Professor von Volt had invented in case of emergencies!

I grabbed a flashlight and headed down to the basement.

I counted

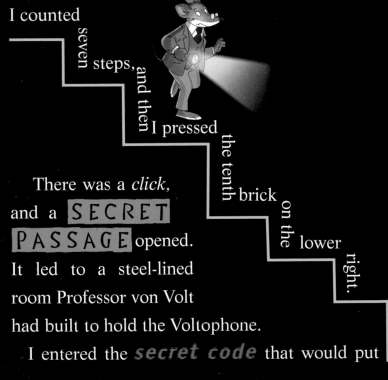

seven steps, and then I pressed

There was a *click,* and a SECRET PASSAGE opened. It led to a steel-lined room Professor von Volt had built to hold the Voltophone.

the tenth brick on the lower right.

I entered the *secret code* that would put

me in touch with my old friend, but he didn't answer.

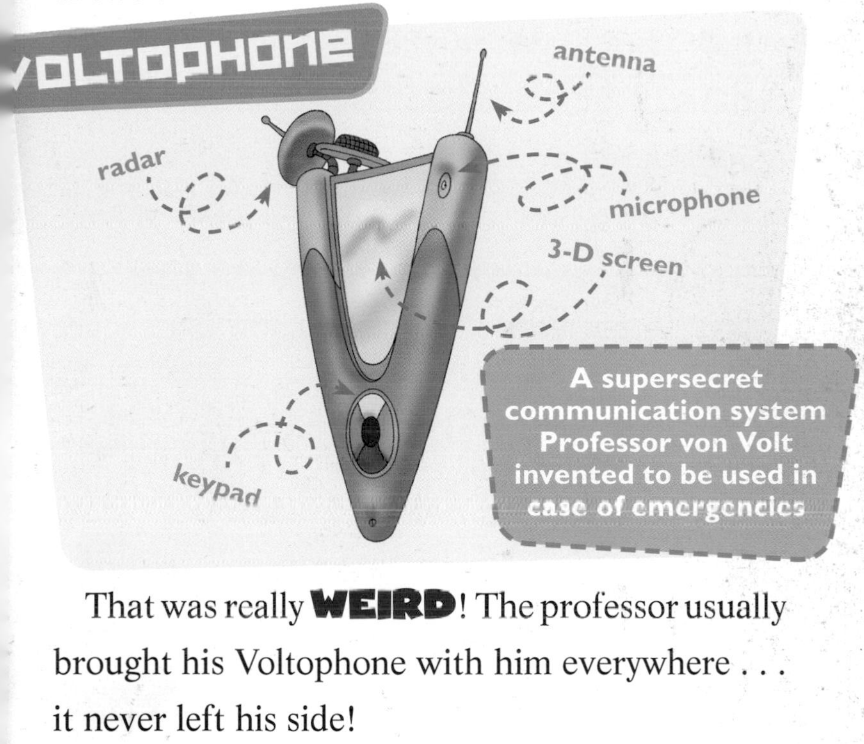

VOLTOPHONE

radar

antenna

microphone

3-D screen

keypad

A supersecret communication system Professor von Volt invented to be used in case of emergencies

That was really **WEIRD**! The professor usually brought his Voltophone with him everywhere . . . it never left his side!

Worried, I decided to go look for him. I immediately headed for New Mouse City's **EGYPTIAN MOUSEUM**. I hoped he'd gone to see Professor Cyril B. Sandsnout, since he'd said Professor Sandsnout was in **desperate** need of help.

But when I got to the mouseum, Professor Sandsnout was there **ALONE**. He was pacing around the empty lobby.

I scampered over to greet him. "Good evening, Professor Sandsnout! I'm looking for Professor von Volt. I thought he'd be here, since he left me a message that he was going to help you," I said **ANXIOUSLY**. "In the meantime, what do you need help with? I'm sure our friend will be here shortly . . ."

I smiled at him encouragingly and tried to keep calm and scurry on. But I was still really, reeeeaaally worried about Professor von Volt.

"Shhh, follow me to my office. There are a lot of spies around!" Professor Sandsnout whispered.

He led me past a statue of **Bastet**, the cat goddess. For a moment, I thought she was gazing at me and licking her whiskers!

Then we crossed the great Sphinx hall. For a moment, I felt like the Sphinxes were staring at me as if I were a tasty treat!

Shhh!

Finally, we passed the Sarcophagus room. For a moment, it seemed like the mummies were glowering at me through their dressings!

I feel like I'm... being watched...

Rancid rat hairs! You've probably realized it by now: Ancient Egypt makes me nervous! Why? Because I'm . . . umm . . . allergic to mummies!

Ancient Egypt makes me nervous!

I didn't feel SAFE till I got to the

THE EGYPTIAN MOUSEUM

7

8

9

10

11

12

1. Entrance
2. The Mummy with No Name
3. Papyrus Room
4. Canopic Jar Room
5. Sphinx Hall
6. Stairway
7. Scarab Room

8. Sarcophagus Room
9. Jewel Room
10. Storage Room
11. Cyril B. Sandsnout's office
12. Amulet Room
13. Room of Ramesses II

professor's office. But even there, the door made me a creepy sound when it closed behind me suddenly.

CREEEAAAAK... KABAM!

Still tense because of that, um, mummy allergy, I jumped about three feet in the air. And I ended up **BUMPING** into a pedestal that was holding a superprecious vase that had belonged to Akhenaten. ①

I tried to keep it from falling, but I crashed into

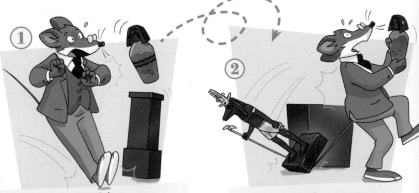

① I knocked into a superprecious vase that belonged to Akhenaten.

② I made the statue of Sebek fall . . . and it crushed my tail!

the statue of Sebek, the crocodile god, which fell to the ground and *crushed* my tail. ② **YEE-OUCH, THAT WAS PAINFUL!**

Squeaking in pain, I began to hop around the room. That's when I accidentally knocked over a collection of emerald scarabs! ③

Finally, I found a pitcher of fresh water and dipped my tail in it to soak. ④ **WHEW!**

"Mr. Stilton, calm down!" Cyril B. Sandsnout ordered. "Sit on that chair and please, **DON'T MOVE**!"

Then he began to tell me his tale.

I knocked over a collection of precious emerald scarabs.

Finally I was able to soak my tail!

A MESSAGE FROM THE PAST

Professor Sandsnout quickly explained that one of his academic **RIVALS**, Professor Martin McSnootersnout, had accused him of preserving fake artifacts in his mouseum!

"I asked Professor von Volt for help defending the mouseum's reputation. If he can prove that Cleopatra's* mirror, our most important relic, is authentic, all McSnootersnout's accusations would be refuted! You see, some historians believe this object contains a mysterious message Julius Caesar wrote to Cleopatra. As the centuries passed, the message was lost. We need to find it by next week, when I'm holding an important conference about ancient Egypt." He sighed deeply. "Come with

*Cleopatra VII was the last queen of ancient Egypt.

me, I'll show you the mirror."

Professor Sandsnout led me to the Cleopatra room, where there were many objects that had belonged to the famouse *queen*. Among them was a very precious ancient mirror made of a thin plate of waxed bronze. On the handle, there was an etching of the **goddess Maat**. I was squeakless: The mirror was **MAGNIFICENT**!

"This mirror is truly worthy of a queen!" I exclaimed.

The ancient Egyptians drew the goddess Maat as a woman whose head was adorned with a feather. She was the goddess of truth and justice, and her job was to bring order to the world.

"You're absolutely right, Mr. Stilton. It is said that after Cleopatra, this mirror belonged to other **FAMOUSE MOUSELETS** of the past, including **BORTE**, Genghis Khan's wife and grand empress of Mongolia; Beatrice, the true love of the esteemed Italian poet Dante Alighieri; and even Queen Elizabeth I of England."

Professor Sandsnout opened the glass case and gave me the honor of ADMIRING Cleopatra's mirror up close. My heart skipped a **beat** as I took it gently in my paws: It was a very rare ancient object.

At that moment, something incredible happened: A *message* from Professor von Volt appeared on the surface of the mirror!

As I gazed at it, the writing VANISHED without a trace.

HELP ME!
I'M A PRISONER
IN THE PAST!
— PAWS
VON VOLT

In a flash, I realized what had happened. Desperate to help his friend, the professor had gone on a *journey through time* all alone, and now he was in **DANGER**!

It was all my fault! Why had I unplugged my phone? If I hadn't gotten sick, my friend wouldn't be in **TROUBLE**!

Quickly, I said good-bye to Cyril B. Sandsnout. "Now I understand everything, but I'm afraid I'm in a **RUSH**. Excuse me, I must go!"

Professor Sandsnout grabbed me by the

Sniffle, sniffle!

jacket, crying desperately, "Pleeeeeaaaase, don't leave meeeee, I need your help!"

"Don't worry, I'm going to look for the professor! And together we'll **PROVE** the mirror is real!" I assured him.

Then I scurried away in search of a quiet place.

I hid in a dark alley and took off the CHAIN that I wear around my neck. On it is a key and a steel CAPSULE.

I remembered what the professor had told me: "Geronimo, always keep this around your neck. Open the capsule only if you fear something terrible has happened to me. Inside you will find very specific instructions. Follow them to the letter!"

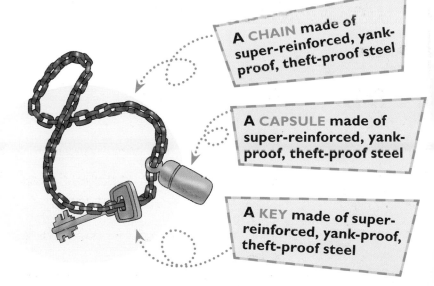

A CHAIN made of super-reinforced, yank-proof, theft-proof steel

A CAPSULE made of super-reinforced, yank-proof, theft-proof steel

A KEY made of super-reinforced, yank-proof, theft-proof steel

My whiskers were **twitching** with tension as I unscrewed the steel capsule. It contained a **rolled-up note** that I read very carefully.

The note gave me instructions to find von Volt's **supersecret** laboratory. Once there, I could reach him in the past!

I needed help, so I grabbed my CELL PHONE and tried to contact all my relatives

Dear Geronimo,

If you are reading this letter, it means I am in danger! Follow these directions and you will reach my secret laboratory. My nephew, Dewey, will meet you there. Ask him for help reaching me in the past.

Use the key from the chain to open the manhole beneath the monument in the center of Singing Stone Plaza. Go underground and take the second right and the third left. You will see a stain in the shape of a were-rat on the wall.

and friends. But NO ONE answered!

So I decided to leave a MESSAGE for everyone: "I need help! I'll wait for you at Singing Stone Plaza. Meet me there at midnight on the dot."

I had a feeling the adventure that was about to begin would be a much more *dangerous* journey than usual. Unfortunately, I was right, but I didn't find out for sure until later . . .

Turn right and then take the metal stairway (*be careful not to fall* — it's very slippery). Count 75 steps through the sludge and you'll find a brick wall — don't hit your snout!

Look for a brick with a *V* on it. Push it and you will reach my secret laboratory. See you soon!

Professor Paws von Volt

P.S. Ask your family and friends for help. It's dangerous traveling through time alone!

IN THE PROFESSOR'S SECRET LABORATORY

That night, I was in Singing Stone Plaza at **midnight** on the dot. The city was still covered in snow, and the streets were deserted.

The bells in City Hall began to strike twelve: Dong! Dong! Dong! Dong! Dong! Dong! Dong! Dong! Dong! Dong! Dong! Dong!

But there was no sign of my friends or family. NO ONE had come to help me!

Suddenly, two *mysterious* figures popped out from behind the monument. At first I almost fainted from fright, but then I realized it was **Wild Willie** and a rodent with dark eyes and long fur that was as smooth as silk.

I couldn't believe it. It was Maya,* one of the most **fascinating** rodents I've ever known.

*Read about my first adventure with Maya in my book *Rumble in the Jungle.*

Wild Willie

WHO HE IS: An archaeologist and lover of adventure. He calls himself a "treasure hunter," but he's not interested in money. In fact, he donates all the archaeological treasures he finds to New Mouse City's mouseums.

SPORTS: He is an avid sportsmouse and practices everything from karate to mountaineering.

HIS PASSION: Solving mysteries

HIS INTEREST: Involving Geronimo (whom he likes to refer to as a "rookie") in his amazing adventures!

HIS MOTTO: "Are you ready for an adventure?" If you are foolish enough to answer yes, he'll reply, "Go with the adventure!"

HIS HOBBIES: He studies languages of the past.

HIS SECRET: He has a tattoo of a red dragon on his forepaw.

Maya

WHO SHE IS: Wild Willie's cousin. She's an archaeology student.

SPORTS: She plays them all, especially anything extreme!

HER PASSION: Accompanying Wild Willie on his adventures

HER INTEREST: Collecting souvenirs from her travels

HER MOTTO: "Nothing is impossible!"

HER HOBBIES: Reading adventure novels

HER SECRET: . . . It's a secret!

I must confess, I have a little **crush** on her.

I tried to *kiss* her paw, but she just took my paw in hers and shook it energetically. "Hey, rookie, you remember me, right? I'm **Maya**, Wild Willie's cousin. Are you still as SOFT as cream cheese?" She looked me in the eye. "You look paler than mozzarella. You're not **afraid**, are you?"

Hi, rookie!

I was trying to avoid making a bad impression! "Umm, a-f-fraid? Me? N-no, th-this is how my snout always looks," I stuttered. "Anyway, my name is *Geronimo*, not 'rookie.'"

Maya peered at me. "Well, you look afraid to me. Your **whiskers** are shaking, and your fur is WHITER than mold on Brie!"

I broke like a rusty spring on an old mousetrap.

"Okay, I'm a total 'fraidy mouse, all right! You popped out of nowhere, and it's the middle of the night, and I got scared, okay?!"

Wild Willie winked at her. "Told ya, Cuz," he said. "The rookie is a **TOTAL SCAREDY-RAT**!" Then he turned to me. "Okay, that's enough chitchat! You said you needed HELP . . ."

"Yes, yes, that's right!" I replied. "We need to find Professor von Volt's **secret** laboratory! FOLLOW ME!"

Using the professor's key, I opened the manhole and led them into the tunnels under the city.

It was so dark down there!

Bad Impression #1

Luckily, Wild Willie pulled some helmets and flashlights out of his bag. "Check it out, rookie. *Always be prepared!*"

Once we reached the end of the stairway, I followed the professor's instructions.

We took the second tunnel on the right, and then the third on the left. I saw a spooky shadow on the wall and let out a shriek of fear (*bad impression #1*). Then I realized it was the STAIN in the shape of the were-rat the professor had mentioned . . . phew!

I turned right and found the slippery staircase. I immediately slipped and hit my tail (*bad*

Bad Impression #2

Bad Impression #3

impression #2). Then I **TRUDGED** through the sludge, counting **SEVENTY-FIVE STEPS**, until I hit my snout (*bad impression #3*) against the brick with the letter **V** on it.

At that point, the secret passage opened, and we found ourselves in Professor von Volt's *laboratory*!

As soon as we entered the lab, an eardrum-bursting **siren** sounded, a blinding light *flashed*, and we found ourselves hanging from the ceiling, caught in a **NET** like tuna in a fishermouse's boat!

A rodent appeared below us. "Who are you? What are you doing here?" he asked suspiciously.

"I'm Stilton, *Geronimo Stilton*, and these are my friends," I gasped. "Professor von Volt told me how to reach his secret lab."

As soon as he heard my name, the rodent apologized. "Oh! I'm sorry about the *booby traps* — you can never be too careful! I'm Dewey

RED ALERT! RED ALERT! RED ALERT!

RED ALERT! RED ALERT! RED ALERT!

INTRUDERS! INTRUDERS! INTRUDERS!

INTRUDERS! INTRUDERS! INTRUDERS!

von Volt, the professor's nephew."

He turned to a funny little robot hiding behind him. "Roborat-8, free the PRISONERS!"

With a tinny laugh, the robot extended a long mechanical arm equipped with extra-large scissors. He cut the cord holding the net, and we fell to the ground in a tangle of tails.

KABAM!

AND IF WE DON'T REMATERIALIZE?

Dewey was full of apologies. He helped us to our paws and led us to his study. "*ROBORAT-8*, prepare a pot of hot tea!" he ordered.

"Do this, do that, go here, go there! Do I have to do **everything** around here?!" the little robot grumbled.

He offered me a cup. I took a gulp and then spit it out, disgusted. "This tastes **terrible**!"

Roborat 8 laughed. "*HEE, HEE, HEE*, what a ridicumouse robot I am! I used salt instead of sugar. Did you know that I'm an authorized experimental prototype? That means that I'm authorized to make **MISTAKES**!"

My whiskers twitched. I had a feeling he had salted my tea on purpose! But I decided to let it go. I had much more serious things to think about.

In the meantime, Dewey was telling me about Professor von Volt. "My uncle tried many times to reach you, Mr. Stilton. But when he couldn't squeak with you, he left **by himself**. He should have returned by now! I'm very **worried** about him. He's too old to be traveling through time alone . . ."

At that point, a **tear** ran down my snout. "Dewey, your uncle is in danger. He is trapped in the past! He's probably back in the time of Cleopatra. He sent me a **message** on a mirror that belonged to the ancient queen. It's all my fault he's missing! I should have gone instead of him . . . I never should have unplugged my phone, even if I did have a **terrible** cold!"

Wild Willie put a paw on my shoulder. "Rookie, as my great-great-grandma Wild Wilhelmina used to say, there's no point crying over spilled fondue. The important thing now is to **take action**!"

"You're right," I squeaked decidedly. "It's time to embark on a new journey through time. I will save my friend Professor von Volt! Do you want to come with me?"

"**Yes!**" Maya and Wild Willie cried.

But Dewey sighed. "Unfortunately, the new time-travel machine isn't quite ready. Using it could be very **risky** . . ."

"Could we use an old one?" I asked.

He shook his snout. "**IMPOSSIBLE!** My uncle left with the Paw Pro Portal, the Rodent Relocator is **broken** from the last journey, and the Mouse Mover 3000 —"

Roborat-8 interrupted him. "That's such an outdated model. It's not worthy of a latest-model experimental prototype like myself!"

Dewey sighed. "Our best bet is to use the brand-new time machine . . . *but I don't know if it works!*" he replied. "I'm still working out some calculations. And there hasn't been any time to **TEST** it . . ."

Dewey led us to another area of the laboratory, where a mysterious machine was hidden under a cloth. Delicately, Dewey lifted the cover and **UNVEILED** it. "Ladies and gentlemice, here it is . . . the *TAIL TRANSPORTER*! Professor von Volt's latest invention!"

TAIL TRANSPORTER

NAME: Tail Transporter

SPEED: 3 ratillion times the speed of light

SEATS: 6 mice maximum

MATERIAL: 24 karat gold

DIMENSIONS: The sphere has a diameter of 50 mouse tails.

The surface is gilded in a special material that absorbs and recycles cosmic photon energy and multiplies it 700 ratillion times!

The Tail Transporter can shrink and can be worn on a chain around a rodent's neck

Cushioned interior
for a soft landing

RAT-O-RAY
Turns the crew to dust,
and then rematerializes
them in the past.

Roborat-8 is the onboard computer for the Tail
Transporter, and he must be present in order for
it to activate. During the journey through time, the
Rat-o-Ray will dematerialize the crew — turning
mice into dust. A few moments later, the team then
rematerializes in the past.

The inside of the Tail Transporter is cushioned to
guarantee a soft landing when the effects of the
Rat-o-Ray are completed.

"This time machine has a special surface that absorbs COSMIC PHOTON energy and multiplies it seven hundred ratillion times!" Dewey said proudly. "When you are ready to leave, a RAT-O-RAY will dematerialize you, turning you into mouse DUST. After a few seconds, it will (maybe . . . probably!) rematerialize you in the past."

My tail was twisting in terror. "Rat-o-Ray? Mouse d-d-dust? What if it, um, DOESN'T rematerialize us?"

"Well, in that case, I will be sure to have a lovely FUNERAL for all of you," Dewey said, waving a paw casually.

"F-f-funeral?" I squeaked. "Um, I'm sorry, I'm ALLERGIC to tombs. They make my fur break out in hives. So . . . okay, I'll see you later, thanks!"

But Maya grabbed me by the tail before I could slink away. "Oh no, you're staying right here! My cousin is right, rookie, you *are* softer than cream cheese. You're a hopeless 'fraidy mouse!"

I was ashamed. She was right, and I was making another **bad impression** on that courageous and fascinating rodent.

I blushed to the roots of my fur. "It's not that I'm actually afraid . . . I w-was just, er, pretending. I love to j-joke around . . ."

"Oh, sure, okay, whatever you say," Maya said, rolling her eyes.

Ummm . . .

You're a hopeless 'fraidy mouse!

GO WITH THE ADVENTURE!

I tried to change the subject. "So, Dewey, is that Ray-Rat-thingy really necessary?"

"The **RAT-O-RAY**? It is absolutely essential!" he answered. "It will make you light enough to you can travel *QUICKLY* through time and space. But don't worry, Mr. Stilton: I'm going to send Roborat-8 to help on your journey. He is the latest generation multi-accessory authorized experimental prototype. He has a superstrong memory and is connected to many powerful databases throughout the world. I will reprogram him to check the Rat-o-Ray and the *TAIL TRANSPORTER* miniaturization, and to set the coordinates of your trip. He will be your onboard computer!"

"**What?**" That talkative tin can is coming with

Roborat-8

He is a latest-generation authorized experimental prototype. He has a superpowerful memory and is connected to many databases throughout the world. If necessary, he can supply information of any kind, play videos on an **LED** screen, and shoot useful objects out of his little drawers. He is the onboard computer for the Tail Transporter. He can even shrink himself down to fit easily into a rodent's pocket.

us?" I said, worried. "He's the one controlling the Rat-o-Ray and everything else? Um, now I'm beginning to get **worried**!"

The little *ROBOT* stuck out his tongue at me. "You'd better be nice to me, you 'fraidy mouse!"

Wild Willie quickly stepped between us. "Enough! We are a **team**! No bickering while we're on our *MISSION*. Now shake paws!"

I extended my right paw to Roborat-8, and he extended the **CLAMPS** that were his hands . . .

Hee, hee, hee!

He'd shocked me! And now he was giggling about it!

All my fur was sticking up, but I didn't dare complain

because Maya was **STARING** at me severely.

Dewey gave us all suits made of an experimental **moldable** material that would adapt to the styles of different time periods. He also gave us **SPECIAL** earpieces that would let us understand any language.

"Geronimo, don't forget that the Tail Transporter can shrink down and become a tiny **golden** sphere," Dewey said. "You can wear it around your neck so you always have it, in case you need to leave in a ***hurry***."

He scurried away, then returned pushing a wheelbarrow that held a **GIANT BOOK**. "Here is Roborat-8's instruction manual!"

Instruction manual? It looked like three copies of *Ratster's Unabridged Dictionary* stuck together!

The little robot puffed up his chest. "I'm quite a **complex** model, you see."

Now that we had all the info, I boarded the

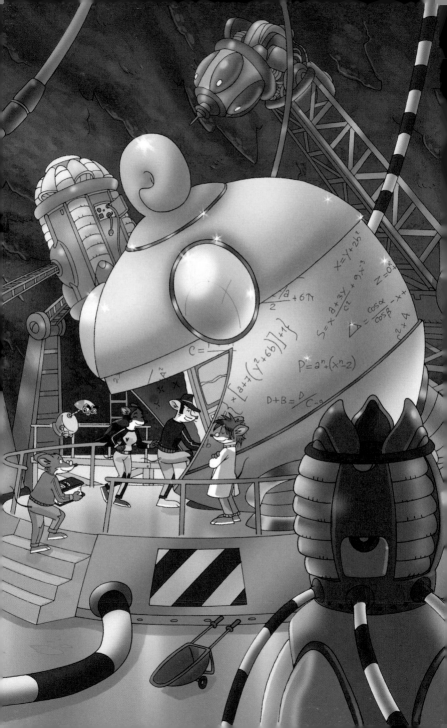

TAIL TRANSPORTER. My tail was trembling with fear, but I tried not to show it.

The door closed behind us.

"Are you ready for an adventure?" Wild Willie hollered.

"Yes!" cried Maya.

"Um," I stammered. "W-well . . . almost. . ."

"I am ready," Roborat-8 said. "I could not be more ready!"

"Go with the adventure!" Wild Willie cried.

The coordinates were set: Alexandria, Egypt, 48 BCE, during the reign of Queen Cleopatra!

Roborat-8 counted down. "**5**. . . **4**. . . **3**. . . **2**. . . **1**. . . Time to dematerialize!"

A ray that looked like **blue goo** surrounded us, and I felt a strange **tingling** followed by a strong itch. I watched as we all dematerialized. After we'd disappeared, I could hear my friends' squeaks echoing in the bluish fog . . .

TO
CLEOPATRA'S
REIGN

48 BCE
ANCIENT EGYPT

FASHION DURING CLEOPATRA'S TIME

Cheese niblets, the ancient Egyptians dressed very strangely! Men wore pleated skirts made of linen, a fabric that's very airy — perfect for the hot climate. Women wore linen, too, in the form of long, fitted dresses under pleated cloaks.

The Egyptians also developed ways to protect their clothing. Soldiers covered their kilts in leather netting, while servants wore nets of beads over their dresses.

Most Egyptians wore sandals made of reeds and papyrus. Some sandals were made of leather sewn together with papyrus twine.

MAKEUP

Both male and female ancient Egyptians wore makeup on their eyes. They used a lead mixture that may have prevented them from catching eye infections. The Egyptians believed makeup gave them the protection of the gods Horus and Ra.

WIGS

In Cleopatra's era, it was very fashionable to wear a wig! Wigs were made of vegetable fibers or natural hair and could be decorated with ribbons and jewels. Queens adorned their wigs with feathers.

HEY, I'M STILL ALIVE!

Suddenly, I heard a strange metallic sound: Screech!

Then the gooey blue fog cleared, and I was able to make out my surroundings.

I felt very itchy, as if all the cells in my body were redistributing themselves. Then I noticed that my body was becoming more and more **SOLID**. I was rematerializing!

But I was still worried: Was I rematerializing the right way? I did a quick check to make sure everything was in the correct place. **Phew!** My tail was exactly where it was supposed to be!

"Are we all still alive?" I murmured.

Roborat-8 **pinched** my ear. "Does that hurt, Geronimoid?"

"**OUCH!**" I shrieked. "Of course it hurts!"

Roborat-8 laughed. "Hee, hee, hee!" Then he **yanked** on one of my whiskers. "What about that?"

"**OOOOWWWW!**" I yelled.

"Oh, it hurts?" the little robot asked innocently. "How bad? A lot, or just a little?"

"**IT HURTS A LOT!**" I yelled.

Then he **SLAPPED** me on the back. "Good news — you're alive!"

"Are you two done **goofing around**?" Maya asked, raising a whisker. "We are here to save Professor von Volt, but you're wasting time like a couple of cheese balls."

Roborat-8 pointed at me. "*IT'S ALL GERONIMO'S FAULT!*"

Wild Willie squeaked up before I had a chance to respond. "Hey, rookie, look over there!" He was pointing to a spot far away on the horizon.

I shaded my **EYES** with one paw. Far in the distance I could see the outline of a city SPARKLING under the hot rays of the sun. "Alexandria, Egypt! The city of the famouse ancient library — the **LEGENDARY** city where Cleopatra lived . . ." I said dreamily.

"You mean the legendary city where Cleopatra *lives,* right?" Maya teased me. "You haven't

Ooooh!

The legendary Alexandria!

Luckily, I'm a grade-A prototype with a built-in fan. Hee, hee, hee!

already forgotten that we're in 48 BCE, have you?"

I **blushed** redder than a cheese rind. "Er, of course I haven't . . . I was just checking to make sure you were paying attention!"

Crusty kitty litter, I had made another **bad impression** on Maya! But I knew I'd redeem myself over the course of our trip. I quickly changed the subject. "So, *let's go*! There's no time to lose."

"Wait! You can't go anywhere **DRESSED** like that," Roborat-8 pointed out. "You all need to change your clothes to **BLEND IN** here."

For once, the little robot was right, so we began to reshape our suits, turning them into **ancient Egyptian** clothes.

Roborat-8 observed us critically as we changed. "Ummmm, that's not quite right!" he barked. "You, shorten that skirt! You, put more **pleats** in that dress! You, fix the *drape* of that cloak!"

After a moment or two, he was satisfied.

Ummm, that's not quite right!

"That's much better! We just need some finishing touches . . . Luckily, I am a Registered Authorized Trial Transport Experimental Robot (**R.A.T.T.E.R.**), and I come with a 3-D scanner and a laser mold-maker!"

Suddenly, Roborat-8 began to *vibrate* like a blender set to supershred. Then he proudly opened one of his drawers. One by one, he shot out . . .

✔ 2 pairs of golden earrings with fake lapis lazuli pendants

✔ I tub of pigment to use as eye makeup

✔ 3 pairs of sandals made of Egyptian-style fake leather

✔ 3 scarab necklaces

✔ 3 rings with seals

✔ 3 wigs with synthetic braids

✔ I superlong piece of striped colored fabric

ACCESSORIES TO BECOME PERFECT ANCIENT EGYPTIANS!

A RING WITH A SEAL

A PAIR OF GOLDEN EARRINGS WITH FAKE LAPIS LAZULI PENDANTS

A TUB OF PIGMENT FOR EYE MAKEUP

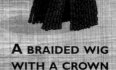

A BRAIDED WIG WITH A CROWN

A LONG PIECE OF STRIPED COLORED FABRIC

A PAIR OF EGYPTIAN-STYLE FAKE LEATHER SANDALS

Roborat-8 snickered. "*HEE, HEE, HEE!* With these accessories, you look like real ancient Egyptians!" Then, much to my surprise, he **JUMPED** on top of my snout and swiftly shrunk himself into my wig!

Roborat-8

"This is my disguise," he explained. "Start marching, mouse!"

I rolled my eyes and obeyed.

But after a few steps, I got a **TERRIBLE** snoutache. Not only was Roborat-8 perched in my wig, but he was also talking nonstop, boasting about his accessories and bossing me around.

"***Faster***, mouse! It's hot under here!"

YOU'VE GOT MORE FLEAS THAN MY CAMEL!

For hours and hours, we TREKKED across the desert, heading toward Alexandria. The city was so far off it seemed like a mirage. And it was so hot!

My paws were burning in the hot sun. The dry desert air irritated my lungs, and a terrible thirst tormented me. My snout felt droopier than string cheese. "Oh, what I wouldn't give for a nice iced cheese!"

Maya twisted her whiskers. "Stop clowning around, rookie! Iced cheese? Have you forgotten we're in the desert back in 48 BCE?"

Jumping gerbils, I had made another BAD IMPRESSION!

But one good thing about already being flushed

red from the heat was that Maya couldn't tell I had turned even **REDDER** with embarrassment!

Just then Wild Willie pointed out some silhouettes moving at the top of a dune . . .

It was a caravan of **MERCHANTS** headed toward us from another trail. As they drew closer, we spotted a clever-looking carpet seller mounted on a mangy camel. Behind him was a sweet-looking mouseling.

Two large, muscular slaves escorted the merchant. They were **ARMED** with long, sharp curved swords, and they glared at us threateningly.

The merchant lifted a paw in greeting. "Peace be with you, foreigners. Are you headed toward Alexandria the beautiful, Alexandria the great, Alexandria the bright?" he called. "My name is Kebel Karpeth and this is my grandson Kebel Babeth. We are merchants from Persia. If you need a carpet, I am the mouse for you! I am the official carpet supplier of Queen Cleopatra! Now, if I may ask, **who** are you and **WHERE** are you going?"

"No, you may not ask, flea-fur!" Roborat-8 shouted from inside my wig.

The merchant glared at me, **offended**. He thought *I* was the one who'd been so rude!

His slaves grabbed the hilts of their swords. "**Grunt!** You offended our master!" they muttered.

"Oh — I'm sorry!" I said. "I meant to say, what a **lovely** camel . . . I'm sure his fur doesn't have fleas!" I pretended to scratch my snout,

desperate to TURN OFF that rude little robot. But I couldn't find the OFF switch! Dewey must have forgotten to attach it . . .

The merchant looked at me suspiciously. "Why are you scratching so much? I think you've got more fleas than my camel does, stranger!"

Maya bowed and squeaked to him politely. "Peace be with you, Kebel Karpeth! We

are ambassadors from afar . . . um, from the land of New Mouse City. We are here to see Queen Cleopatra!"

The merchant turned PALER than a piece of papyrus. "Cleopatra? You mean C-L-E-O-P-A-T-R-A? As in, the queen of Egypt? Oh, by the way, do you need a carpet? You could give her one as a gift! She likes them very much, you know!"

"Yes, Cleopatra. She's the one we seek,"

Maya confirmed. "But we don't need any carpets. Thanks, anyway."

Kebel lowered his squeak and looked around, frightened. "Strangers, if I were you I would think once — twice — even three times before meeting her . . ." he said. "And then I would **TURN BACK**! She is so beautiful, so intelligent, and so powerful, but also . . . so unpredictable, so quick-tempered, so vain, so arrogant, basically . . . **SO VERY DANGEROUS**! And they say she hates ambassadors. The last bunch . . . **Thwack!** She had their snouts cut off!"

"Umm, and the second-to-last bunch? What happened to them?" I asked, my squeak **shaking** in fright.

"The second-to-last ones all **DIED** suddenly from a terrible stomachache . . ." he replied. Then he lowered his squeak even more. By now, he was whispering. "They say she is an expert with **poison**! Be careful, if you care about keeping your fur . . ."

"Grandfather is right," his grandson said, nodding. "Everyone knows she is dangerous. She is **slyer** than a scorpion and more **DEADLY** than an asp!"

"I will give you some advice, friend," the merchant continued. "She likes my carpets very much. They put her in a **good mood**! So I suggest you give her one as a gift. I will cut you a deal!"

I smiled. "Thanks, but we really don't need any carpets."

It was as if he hadn't heard me. ***Quicker*** than a cat chasing a ball of yarn, he'd spread dozens of carpets before us. They were all different **colors** and sizes — and they were all wrapped in clouds of **flies** that stunk of sweaty camel!

"Thank you anyway, but we really don't need them!" I repeated patiently. "However, we would very much like to TRAVEL with your caravan to Alexandria."

Like a good salesmouse, he immediately saw an opportunity. "Of course you can join us, you stubborn stranger with a snout full of fleas who doesn't know how to appreciate beautiful carpets! Just pay the small sum of three silver coins each! During the trip, I will convince you to appreciate my cat-fur carpets, or my name isn't Kebel Karpeth!"

LOOK AT THESE MARVEMOUSE CARPETS. THEY ARE WORTHY OF THE QUEEN!
Mmmm . . .
UM, BEAUTIFU
BUT I DON'T N
CARPETS . .
1
DO YOU WANT TO BUY ONE? I'LL CUT YOU A GOOD DEAL!
Hmm?
THANKS,
BUT I DON'T NEE
ANY CARPETS!
2
MY PRICES ARE EXCEPTIONAL! CHOOSE WHICHEVER BEAUTIFUL ONE YOU WANT!
Hmm . . .
BUT I DON'T NEED A CARPET!
3

YOU DON'T
E THEM, YOU
SAY SO . . .
Umm . . .
WHAT WOULD I DO WITH A CARPET IN THE DESERT?
4
WOULD SPRUCE
YOUR TENT! AND
UR NEIGHBORS
WOULD BE SO
JEALOUS!
Hee, hee!
I DON'T HAVE A TENT OR ANY NEIGHBORS!
5
I CAN
EFINITELY SEE
OU WITH THIS
RPET . . . I WILL
GIVE YOU AN
INCREDIBLE
DISCOUNT!
Ha, ha, ha!
I DON'T WANT ANY CARPETS! I DON'T NEED ANY CARPETS!
OH, ALL
IGHT. YOU
ST HAD TO
SAY SO!
6

THIS CARPET STINKS OF SWEATY CAMEL!

Unfortunately, Kebel Karpeth kept his word. He **pestered** me the entire trip, trying to get me to buy his carpets.

Meanwhile, Wild Willie squeaked with the slaves about **FIGHTING** techniques. Every so often he would chat with Maya, who was sprawled out **COMFORTABLY** on a stretcher.

The road to Alexandria seemed endless, but I

gathered my strength. After all, I had a mission to complete: saving my friend Professor von Volt!

But Alexandria was much farther away than I'd realized. In the desert, it's difficult to calculate distances. The CLEAR air makes everything seem really close, and there aren't many landmarks to help you measure space.

So we scampered and scurried for a long time while the sand and wind DRiED our throats.

But that didn't stop the merchant — he chattered the whole time! He didn't stop squeaking till we crossed a large dune and the tall, solid **WALLS** of the city finally appeared.

"We are here at last. This is so **exciting**!" I murmured dreamily.

We joined a crowd headed toward the gates to the city. After a while, I noticed some rodents were

pointing at us. "Look at those strange merchants riding camels!"

I didn't understand. "What's so strange about riding camels?" I asked.

Roborat-8 **pinched** my ear. "Do I have to **explain** everything?! Listen up!"

He sighed. "Now, we need to find a way to **ENTER** Cleopatra's palace!"

Wild Willie winked

HORSES OR CAMELS?

Camels were known in ancient Egypt. They were domesticated after the Persians reached the Nile in 525 BCE, a long time before Cleopatra lived. But to travel or transport merchandise, the Egyptians preferred horses or donkeys.

at Maya, then said under his breath, "We know how to get in! Here is our plan: We will take advantage of the confusion and hide under the merchant's carpets. If he really does sell carpets to Cleopatra, he'll lead us right to her."

"And then what do we do?" I asked anxiously.

Wild Willie gave me a thwack on the tail that would have knocked over a sarcophagus. "After that, we improvise, rookie!"

We'd reached the city gates. There, guards armed with very sharp swords were checking the belongings of all who wished to enter. They were randomly PLUNGING their swords into things — first a cart of hay, then a sack of grains, then a pile of wood . . . ZIIIIF! ZIIIIP!

I shuddered. "Holey cheese kebabs, this doesn't look good!" I whispered to Wild Willie. "What if the guards stab us through the merchant's carpets?"

Wild Willie shrugged. "Well, then we'll end up as kebabs, just like you said! You know, sooner or later everyone dies. Which reminds me, you've written your will, right, rookie? You've chosen your tombstone, right?"

I protested. "I have NOT written my will! I have NO intention of thinking about my tombstone! And I am certainly not going to end up like a kebab!"

The merchant came to say good-bye. "May good luck be with you. And if you need a carpet, remember me! Got it, you stubborn, flea-ridden stranger?!"

I said good-bye politely. Despite everything, I had taken a liking to him and his lively grandson.

We waited till everyone was distracted, and then we slipped inside the rolled-up carpets.

We were only in three of them, because Roborat-8 had climbed into **my** carpet with me!

He immediately began complaining. "Ugh, it's so **HOT**! Ugh, there's so much dust! Ugh, this carpet **stinks** like a sweaty camel!"

He only piped down when the guards approached, **brandishing** their swords.

"Oh, don't waste your time stabbing these carpets," the merchant said calmly. "They are headed to Cleopatra. If I give her carpets with **HOLES** in them, she won't be happy! And I'll be sure to tell her **WHO** made the holes!"

The guards turned **PaLeR** than a sweaty slice of Swiss. "This changes everything! Please, go right into the city with your wares. We will take you right to the *queen*. She does not love waiting . . ."

Then they scampered ahead of us on the road to **CLEOPATRA'S PALACE**.

Eek . . .
Squeak . . . Ack!

The merchant called two workers to carry the **CARPETS** that concealed us. As they weaved through the crowded streets of Alexandria, I bounced **UP** and **DOWN** with every step. It was like being on a boat. Moldy mozzarella, I was so seasick!

Then they tossed us onto a wagon, and we began to **JOLT** around like rodents on a roller coaster! Rat-munching rattlesnakes, what **wretched** rattling!

I was so seasick!

What wretched rattling!

Finally, they grabbed the carpet on each end, and we began to *swing* back and forth like a seesaw. **Cheese niblets, I was so terribly nauseous!**

Plus, the carpet smelled like sweaty camel, and it was full of **fleas**! I wanted to scratch, but I couldn't. I was all rolled up like a **cheese** dumpling . . . and, unfortunately, I was the stuffing!

The two workers were **COMPLAINING**, too. "Yee-ouch, this carpet is so heavy! And it stinks like a smelly camel!"

"Stop, I need to scratch! This isn't a carpet, this is a heap of fleas, lice, and . . ."

"And bedbugs! You forgot the **bedbugs**!"

I was so terribly nauseous!

"No, I didn't forget them, how could I? They're biting me all over!"

Suddenly, I realized I had to **sneeze**. I tried to hold it in, but after a few minutes, I just couldn't.

"Aaachoooooooo!"

"**BLEƒƒ YOU!**" both workers cried at once.

Luckily, each of them thought the **other** had sneezed! I was saved — at least for now . . .

Just a moment later, though, my throat began to itch, and I had a coughing fit!

Cough, cough, cough!

I was sure I'd be discovered, but they both called out at once, "What a **NASTY** cough! You really should take care of that!"

Each of them thought the **other** had coughed . . . so once again I was saved!

Even though I was curled up like a cheese roll inside the carpet, I was able to glimpse a bit of the city. We passed through crowded streets with stands full of **MULTICOLORED** goods and spices that filled the air with *exotic* scents.

Hundreds of languages were being spoken: Greek, Latin, Egyptian, Hebrew . . . Alexandria was truly an enormouse city!

Roborat-8 began to lecture me. "My dear *GERONIMOID*, take this opportunity to educate yourself! Here is the most up-to-date information on the history of Alexandria. Good thing I'm here to explain things to you. I'll do what I can to bring you up to my level!"

I tried to shush him. That *snooty* garbage-can-on-wheels was going to get us caught with his boisterous bragging!

"How can I **turn you off**? There must be a way to keep you quiet!" I muttered.

1. The Island of Pharos
2. The Temple of Isis Pharia
3. The Pharos of Alexandria (the Lighthouse)
4. The Temple of Isis Lochia
5. Royal Palace
6. Theater
7. Museum
8. Library
9. Racecourse
10. Cleopatra's Palace

Roborat-8 giggled. "Maybe there is, maybe there isn't! But if there were, I certainly wouldn't tell you! Hee, hee, hee!"

Luckily, there was a lot of COMMOTION around us, and no one heard his NONSTOP boasting — except for me. Unfortunately, I could hear him all too well!

When we reached the Pharos of Alexandria, a famouse lighthouse, he fell silent for a moment so he could ADMIRE it. But his silence only lasted a few seconds. Then he began spitting out information again. BLAH. BLAH. BLAH . . .

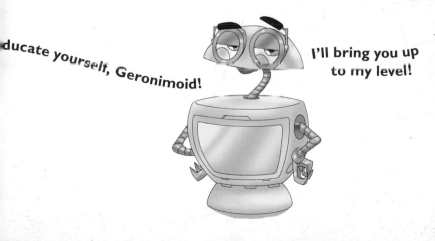

ducate yourself, Geronimoid!

I'll bring you up to my level!

I stopped listening. I was too excited: Before me lay one of the **Seven Wonders of the World**!* And in the face of all that beauty, you don't need words.

I drank in that incredible sight. The marble of the enormouse lighthouse stood out so white against the sparkling blue water.

By now, the sky was turning to dusk, and the first STAR of the evening twinkled timidly in a corner of the sky. The beam of the lighthouse began to shine to guide the sailors to shore. The palace of Cleopatra lay right before our snouts!

---

*The Seven Wonders of the World are monuments that ancient writers considered the most remarkable ever created by humanity: the Hanging Gardens of Babylon, the Colossus of Rhodes, the Mausoleum of Halicarnassus, the Temple of Artemis at Ephesus, the Lighthouse of Alexandria, the Statue of Zeus at Olympia, and the Pyramids of Giza.

Cleopatra's palace sank into the Mediterranean Sea after a series of earthquakes and tsunamis more than a thousand years ago. The archaeological remains are all submerged. The Egyptian government would like to construct a giant underwater museum so everyone can admire the ruins, but work on the project has not yet begun. This reconstruction is the product of Geronimo Stilton's imagination!

ARE THESE MICE INCLUDED IN THE PRICE?

I didn't know if I should be happy because my **dreadful discomfort** was about to end or terrified because we had reached Cleopatra's palace.

Would the queen have our snouts chopped off? Would she feed us to her **ROYAL BEASTS**? Or would she poison us and leave us to squeak "so long, world"?!

I was about to have a panic attack, but I gathered my **strength** and thought of my dear friend Professor von Volt.

As the workers carried us toward the throne room, my teeth began to **chatter** so loudly, I was afraid everyone would hear . . .

Click clack! **Click** Clack!
Clack clack! Click! clac

To dull the sound, I put a **PAW** in my mouth. But a moment later, the workers threw the carpet to the ground, which made me **BITE** down hard on my paw.

It was so painful, I couldn't help crying out, "**YEE-OUUUCH!**"

This time, I was sure I'd be in trouble, but they both cried, "**SORRY!**"

Each of them thought they had crushed the **other's** paw. What a couple of cheesebrains!

While the merchant was waiting for **Cleopatra** to receive him, we stayed rolled up in our carpets in a corner.

From my hiding place, I could hear an imperious **female** squeak. "Let's get on with the fashion show. I need to choose a new outfit for my next speech."

At those words, flute **music** began, along with the rhythm of a tambourine. A few lavishly dressed **mouselets** began to parade around in front of me.

As they passed in front of the queen, she

commented impatiently, "**NO!** That one is too long! **NO!** That one is too short! **NO! NO! NO! NO! NO!** That one doesn't work. It's not that it's too long or too short, it just has no personality!"

She kept going. "That one has too many **clashing** colors! That one's plainer than papyrus! Call the court tailor — I have some words for him! If he doesn't show me something better immediately, I'll feed him to my **royal beasts**!"

Her pawmaidens rushed to summon the tailor. **Poor rat** . . . I wouldn't have wanted to be in his sandals!

"Next! You, with the carpets — let me see your goods!" Cleopatra ordered.

Before I could wave a whisker, the workers **rolled out** the carpets — with us in them! In a split second, we were lying at the foot of Cleopatra's throne.

Finally, I could see her snout. She was a rodent with eyes as **deep** and dark as the night. Her fur was golden like the desert sand. She was **fascinating** and beautiful. And it was clear that she was accustomed to commanding and being obeyed!

UNPERTURBED, the queen looked down her snout at us. Her eyes were half closed, shaded by long eyelashes.

MeanWHiLe, everyone around us was murmuring in astonishment.

"OOOH . . ."

"Who are these rodents?"

"What are they doing here?"

The **GUARDS** were already headed toward us, but Cleopatra stopped them. "Are these mice included in the price?" she asked the carpet seller.

Kebel Karpeth shook his snout. "My great queen, I wasn't . . . it's not my fault! I don't know how they ended up in there!"

Cleopatra waved a paw dismissively. "No matter, three more slaves are always convenient!"

So the master of the slaves stepped toward us,

Ha, ha, ha!

Help!

cracking his whip. *Thwack!*

"On your paws, **SLACKERS**!" he snarled. "What are your skills?"

He flicked his WHIP toward Wild Willie, but my friend quickly grabbed it by the tip. With a tug, he flipped the master onto his back.

Then Wild Willie passed Maya the whip, and she cracked it at the master's paws three times.

THWACK! THWACK! THWACK!

Everyone laughed (except the slave master, obviously!). As he stepped back, tail between his paws, Cleopatra turned to Maya. "Hmm . . . you seem PLUCKY!" Then she looked over at Wild Willie. "And you seem strong! But *how* **STRONG** are you?"

Thwack!

Thwack!

Thwack!

Wild Willie bowed, half closing his SPARKLY green eyes. "My queen, I am ready to take on anymouse you put before me!"

A look of satisfaction passed across Cleopatra's snout. "Very well. The fighting shall begin at once. It's been a while since we've had any *fun* here at the palace . . ."

Then she clapped her paws, and three slaves as large as cheetahs and with paws as big as lions strode into the room. They POUNCED on Wild Willie, but he knocked them all down in a flash. He used a **secret** ancient karate technique* — he's a real pro.

Cleopatra gave him a bewitching smile. "You not only seem **STRONG**, you really *are*! You're handsome, too! You will become my **PeRSoNaL bodyguaRD**, along with her right there . . ."

Then she stopped and looked Maya up and

*The technique is called *tuite*, and you can learn about it in my book *The Way of the Samurai*.

down from snout to tail. "By the way, who is she? She isn't your girlfriend, is she?"

"No, no, I'm his cousin," Maya said quickly.

"Good," the queen replied. Only then did she turn to me. I trembled under the scrutiny of that imperious gaze. "**YOU** — what do you know how to do? You look a bit feeble compared to your friends!"

I hesitated for a second too long. "I, um . . ." I began.

Cleopatra got impatient. "If you don't know how to do anything, I will **feed** you to the royal beasts!" she snapped. "At least you will be **USEFUL** for something, and I will save on their royal grub. Those cheeseballs are always so hungry!"

MYSTERY IN THE PALACE

At that point, I answered quickly, but I was so **SCARED** that I stuttered. "N-no, n-no, don't f-feed me to the b-beasts! I know how to do m-many things: I write, for example!"

"You are a **scribe**?" She sighed. "I'm not interested. I already have too many scribes!"

"I c-could r-read to you!" I offered.

"Not interested — you **stutter** too much!" she replied, waving a paw dismissively.

"Ummm . . . I also know how to solve **mysteries**!" I said desperately.

"Hmm . . . that's interesting! Would you be able to locate something for me? A MIRROR of mine, for example?"

"SAY YES!" Wild Willie whispered.

Maya kicked me. "**Say yes**, you fool, if you want to keep your fur!"

So I stammered, "O-of course . . . **YES**, my queen!"

"Well, we'll see! If you fail, I could still feed you to my **LIONS**," Cleopatra declared.

I took a deep breath. I was determined not to fail. I pulled out a **notebook**. "My queen, describe the object you lost, and I will find it for you."

"Ah, so you were telling the truth. You do know how to write! Good. If you practice, you could become my **personal** scribe," Cleopatra said.

I noticed the head scribe was glaring at me. Putrid cheese puffs, I had made a fearsome **ENEMY**!

I pretended not to notice. I continued taking notes as Cleopatra described the precious lost object. "It's a very,

The head scribe

very valuable **MIRROR**," she began. "The image of goddess Maat is engraved on the handle, and there's a great lapis lazuli stone encased in it."

Maya, Wild Willie, and I exchanged quick glances. Cleopatra was describing the very **MIRROR** Professor von Volt had written his call for help on — the mirror that had, many centuries later, ended up in the Egyptian Mouseum!

Meanwhile, Cleopatra was making a solemn announcement to her attendants. "Listen up, everyone. This mouse must **LOOK** everywhere for my mirror. You must help him and give him access to all the rooms. Answer all his questions and give him all the information he asks for, understand? Otherwise there will be trouble!"

Then she signaled for me to approach the throne. "Lowly rodent, that mirror is quite

precious to me," she said under her breath, so that only I could hear. "My adorable little Caesar* gave it to me, and he hid a **MESSAGE** for me in it. A very, umm, personal message."

My whiskers quivered. She was talking about the same *hidden message* Cyril B. Sandsnout had mentioned! That was the **proof** we needed to save the reputation of the mouseum! Finally, we knew where it was!

Cleopatra's squeak pulled me from my thoughts. "If you find the mirror, you shall be covered in **GOLD** and honors. But if you fail, I will feed you to the royal beasts! When they are finished, there will be nothing left of you to **mummify**!"

I **GULPED**. What a terrifying thought! I didn't want to be devoured by royal beasts!

Before Cleopatra left, she handed me a ring. "With this **RING**, you

*The great general Gaius Julius Caesar lived between 100 and 44 BCE. He ruled Rome and led many military ventures, among which was conquering Gaul and Egypt.

I looked in the royal kitchen . . .

I looked in the royal gardens . . .

will be granted access to any chamber in my palace you wish to see," she said.

Then she **swept** out of the room with her entourage behind her. Her new bodyguards, Maya and Willie, brought up the rear.

I let out a **SIGH** of relief. For the moment, I was still alive, and not only that, I had a great excuse to snoop around and look for Professor von Volt. I had the **OFFICIAL** authorization of the queen!

So I inspected the royal kitchen, where the royal banquets were prepared. I

visited the royal gardens, full
of beautiful royal flowers.
The guards even opened
the royal bedroom for me,
so I could carefully check
there as well . . . But I
didn't find a single **trace**
of the mirror, or of Professor

**I even looked in
the royal ponds!**

von Volt. Not even in the royal ponds,
home of the queen's royal animal companions!

After days of searching uselessly, I lost all
HOPE. I was certain I'd end up as food for the
ROYAL BEASTS.

I decided to take a break. I went to visit the
famouse **library** of Alexandria. It was every
bookmouse's dream . . .

The library of Alexandria in Egypt was built in the third century BCE. It was the largest library in antiquity and one of the main cultural centers in the world. The library was ultimately destroyed, many believe by a fire set by Julius Caesar's forces during his occupation of Alexandria in 48 BCE. But no one knows for certain how it met its fate.

Pro-Fes-Sor . . . von Volt!

I was more excited than a hungry rat at a cheese buffet. I gazed in wonder at the thousands of **papyrus** scrolls arranged on the library's shelves. They were the works of the GREATEST poets, philosophers, and scientists of antiquity.

Even Roborat-8, who was hidden in my wig, began to shake from impatience and excitement. "Crackling circuits! There's so much **information** in this place! Oh, if only I could scan all these papyruses, I would be the richest robot in the world!"

Then he fainted — I mean **crashed** — from all the excitement. At last, he was silent. Whew!

A rodent with a **KIND** and intelligent gaze approached me. He stared at my glasses in amazement, and then he greeted me politely.

"Hello, stranger! My name is **BIBLI-O-RAT** and I am the librarian here. Can I help you?"

I immediately struck up a **FRiENDSHiP** with him. He enthusiastically showed me the library's many, many prized works. I didn't dare tell him that one day in the not-too-distant future, that enormouse, precious bounty of knowledge would be totally **destroyed**!

When it was time for me to return to the palace, he dragged me behind a bookcase. "I must tell you a *secret*," he said in a low squeak. "But first I must ask you a question. Do you know a certain Pro-Fes-Sor? He's a small rodent who's quite well educated. He knows about many *papyruses*!"

"No, I'm sorry, I don't," I said. "Ah, wait a minute! Is his name **Pro-Fes-Sor . . . von Volt**?"

"Yes, that is his full name! I had almost forgotten. You see, he told me that one day his friend would arrive, and that I would recognize him because

of the transparent butterfly on the tip of his snout,* just like the one you have. You must be that friend . . . and so this is for you."

He cautiously pulled a rolled-up papyrus from the folds of his tunic. It was **SEALED** with a symbol that I recognized: the letter *V*!

My tail was **twitching** with excitement as I unrolled the papyrus. Here's what it said . . .

*No one knows for certain when or where eyeglasses were invented, but scholars believe they first gained widespread use during the Middle Ages. In 48 BCE, they had not yet been invented.

Dear ,

If you are reading this , it means that, thank goodmouse, you were able to arrive safe and sound to the of !

I wanted you to know that I was here and I am proceeding with my journey. If we don't manage to find each other, know that I hid Cleopatra's in the safest of places: the cage!

I buried it under the that contains the they feed on.

Your most affectionate friend,

-Professor von Volt

P.S. In the handle of the mirror, you'll find the message that proves the mirror's authenticity. This will clear Professor Sandsnout of all accusations made against him. I am continuing with my journey to make sure the mirror will reach the present day with the message intact!

When I finished reading, I could barely keep the TEARS from running down my snout. Who knew WHEN I would see my dear friend Professor von Volt again?

Then I shook off my *sadness* and concentrated on my next step. I needed to get the mirror with the message that proved its authenticity and bring it to Cleopatra!

I had to return to the palace and look for the royal cages, where the royal lionesses were held!

As I was SCAMPERING

Oww!

down the street that led to the palace, Roborat-8 powered **BACK UP** again.

Frightened by all my bouncing around, he grabbed my ears and pulled hard.

"**Oww!**" I yelped. I was so startled, I didn't see a hole in the middle of the street. I **tripped** and fell flat on my snout. As I stumbled, the ring with Cleopatra's seal rolled into the **sea**!

"**Crusty kitty litter!**" I yelled. "When Cleopatra finds out, I'll be a feast for her royal beasts! **How in the name of string cheese** am I going to get into the royal cages without that ring?!"

Oopsie!

HEY, YOU! SPHINX FACE!

At the entrance to the royal cages, there was a large GATE that would only open with the seal from Cleopatra's ring. I had to think up a way to get in, and *fast*!

The cages were in the cold, dank basement of the palace. They were lit by torches and there was a strange, **WILD** smell everywhere. What a **CREEPY** place!

As soon as Roborat-8's sensors registered the smell, he jumped off me. "I smell trouble. I'm going to look for help! *BYE-BYE, GERONIMOID!* Try not to get eaten while I'm gone."

"Huh?! Does this seem like a good way to **HELP** me?" I shouted after him. "Come back here, you useless heap of scrap metal!"

But he was already far away, and I was alone!

My whiskers trembling in **TERROR**, I peered through the gate to look for the lion cage. In the semidarkness, I could see the **SNAKE** pit, the crocodile pool, the **SCORPION** tub, the leeches' marsh, the breeding farm for POISONOUS spiders, the aviary for the bloodsucking bats, and, finally . . . the lionesses' cage!

Just then, someone grabbed me by the ear. It was a big, **SCARY** mouse! "Hey, you! Sphinx face!

Hey, you! Sphinx face!

Where do you think you're going? I'm T-Am-Er, and I'm the **BOSS** around here!"

"Umm . . . well, I would be . . . I mean, I meant to say, I am th-the . . ." I stuttered.

The rodent shook me by the ears. "Ah, you're the new **CAGE CLEANER**? I asked so long ago, I didn't think they'd ever send anyone down here . . ."

I lit up. "Yes, I'm him — that's me!"

"Okay, *follow me*!" he ordered. He led me to the cage door and gave me a wooden **SHOVEL** and a **CART**. "Here are the tools of the trade. And look, I want to be generous: I'll even give you a **nose clip**!"

Before I could ask why I needed that, he'd led me to an enormouse cage with golden bars. Inside were the queen's thirty-three **lionesses**. They were circling about, agitated.

I immediately understood what the nose clip

was for: to **PLUG** my snout! Because my job consisted of shoveling enormouse, **superstinky** lioness dung. Oh, what a foul stench!

As soon as I approached the bars, the lionesses roared.

"ROOOOAAAAARRRR!"

I leaped back in **HORROR**.

T-Am-Er snickered. "It's dinnertime! They are

really **StarViNG**! Careful, friend, you don't want to end up becoming their appetizer."

I was about to **faint** from fright. But T-Am-Er grabbed me by the ears before I hit the ground. Then he **thwacked** me on the back so hard he could've knocked over a camel.

"**Calm down**, Sphinx face! While you clean this cage, *they* will be in the one next door," he explained.

He opened a divider that separated the cage from a long corridor LINKED to another cage. The lionesses slowly headed that way, nervously brushing their sides with their tails.

I waited for the last one to leave. Then I opened the door to the cage and scurried in. At last, I could look for Cleopatra's mirror!

I ran toward the food BOWL in the corner, swerving between one piece of dung and the next. I lifted the bowl and began to dig with the shovel that T-Am-Er had given me.

After a few minutes, the shovel hit something hard. It was a decorated wooden chest. I couldn't believe I'd found it so soon! I opened the chest and found it contained Cleopatra's famouse MIRROR.

Quickly, I turned over the lavishly carved handle. The rolled-up message was still inside! It was proof of the mirror's authenticity! It was

My beloved Cleopatra, most beautiful rodent, you are queen of my heart. This mirror is for you. Every time you see your reflection on its shiny surface, you will see yourself as my eyes see you.

Your adoring and adored,
Gaius Julius Caesar

just what we needed to help Cyril B. Sandsnout.

Now we just had to MAKE SURE that the mirror reached our original time with the message still in the handle . . .

I sighed. Oh, how I wanted to go home! But our **MISSION** in the past wasn't finished yet.

It was then that a strange **creaking** interrupted my thoughts . . .

GOOD-BYE, AND THANKS!

I turned suddenly and spotted a silhouette. It was the head scribe! And he had just lifted the divider **separating** me from the ferocious lionesses!

"I won't let you become Cleopatra's personal scribe!" he muttered **wickedly**.

I made a mad dash for the cage exit, but the lionesses had SURROUNDED me!

The head scribe left, giggling. "By the way, they haven't **eaten** yet . . ."

I backed up slowly until I was against the wall of the CAGE. This was a **NIGHTMARE**! After so many adventures and close calls, I was finally going to end my days as **lioness** chow!

But then I heard two sharp cracks of a whip: **Thwack! Thwack!**

It was Wild Willie, Maya, and Roborat-8!

Roborat-8 really had gone to get help! My friends had come to **save me**!

Wild Willie and Maya advanced, cracking their whips, which cleared the **AREA** in front of them. And Roborat-8 hurried between me and the royal beasts while projecting the image of a roaring lion around himself!

The little robot's hologram was very convincing. The lionesses stopped, confused. That gave Wild Willie and Maya time to reach me. They pulled me to my paws, and together we raced to the exit.

The moment we reached safety, I **fainted**!

When I opened my eyes again, I saw Wild Willie and Maya chuckling under their WHISKERS. "Looks like we arrived just in time, rookie!"

Roborat-8 jumped onto my shoulder. "Thank goodmouse you're still alive, Geronimoid! Otherwise, who would I squabble with?!"

"Th-thanks everyone!" I stuttered. "Look what I found: **Cleopatra's mirror!** The message that Caesar wrote to the queen is in the handle. This is what we need to prove the mirror is real and help the **EGYPTIAN MOUSEUM**! We just need to give Cleopatra back the mirror. Then we can leave."

"And Professor von Volt? Where is he?" Roborat-8 asked. A **little tear** of machine oil leaked out of his eyes. "I miss him so!"

The next thing I knew, he was sobbing. He even blew his nose on my tunic! But I let him. Because I'd realized something: Roborat-8 wasn't just a pile of metal and electric circuits. He had a **heart**!

"Professor von Volt left us a message," I said. "He's continued on his *journey*, and he's waiting for us in the future.

I'll bet he's in **BORTE'S** time. She had the mirror after Cleopatra!"

As soon as the little robot **calmed down**, we headed toward the queen's quarters. Cleopatra received us right away. When she saw the mirror, her snout lit up. "Oh, so you found it at last! Good work!"

But when she gazed at herself in the mirror, she shouted, "**Aaaaah! A pimple!** How dare you give me a mirror now? You've ruined my **ROYAL MOOD**! I will feed you to the royal beasts after all!"

"Friends, it's **TIME TO GO**!" I cried.

We scampered away before she could send her guards after us. Breathlessly, we **ran** through the long halls of the palace. We soon found ourselves **alone** in a large chamber.

I took the small golden SPHERE and rubbed it between my paws, and the Tail Transporter returned to its original size.

The RAT-O-RAY started working the minute we boarded. And so began our journey to meet Borte!

Scurry up, let's go!

I'm Sorry, I'm Not a Shaman!

After what seemed like forever, I once again felt a funny tingling all over . . .

We were rematerializing!

We did a quick check to make sure our paws and tails and snouts had all ended up in the right places. Then we began to mold our clothes and transform them into **DEELS**, the traditional Mongol clothing.

Roborat-8 added the final touches to our outfits: jewels, hair clips, and hems of fake fur. He gave me long **WHISKERS** pointed downward, in Mongol fashion. (Wild Willie didn't need any — he had them already!) Maya plaited her fur into long **braids** and tied them with leather cords.

As soon as we were ready, Roborat-8 shrank

FASHION IN GENGHIS KHAN'S TIME

Mongols wore comfortable warm clothing to help them brave the freezing cold of the steppe — their vast region of dry grassland and extreme temperature ranges. *Brrr!*

The temperature in winter could reach 50 degrees below zero. Squeak! Even in these conditions, though, the Mongols did not give up their elegance. Their clothing was covered with fine decorations.

My deel is warm and really soft!

Does this braided fur-do look good on me?

What a mouserific outfit!

DEEL: This was a long gown made of patterned silk in bright colors. In winter, it was lined with wool to keep the wearer warm. Men wore a sash in a contrasting color.

GUTAL: These decorated boots had turned-up toes, which allowed people to ride comfortably and walk easily in the grass . . . even through the snow!

WOMEN'S CLOTHING: Women also wore *deels* to keep warm.

STRIPS OF FABRIC: Tied around the waist, these kept the *deel* in place but could also become useful pockets.

CURLED TOES: There are several possible reasons why Mongols wore shoes with curled toes. One is that because the bottom of a shoe with a curled toe covers less surface area on the ground than a regular shoe, the wearer has a lower potential to harm plants and small animals with each step.

HATS: These were lined with fur. On warm days, the sides were rolled up and tied in the back.

down and hid under my fur hat.

We heard strange noises coming from outside. I **SHUDDERED** with dread.

When the Tail Transporter opened, I let out a squeak of **terror**. A few yards away, on the other side of a hill, stood a group of horsemice with long whiskers. They were led by a female rodent with really long braids. She was dressed in WHITE fur, and her eyes were black and **intense**. She had the expression of someone who knows how to get respect.

I had just enough time to shrink down the *TAIL TRANSPORTER* and hang it around my neck before the group of Mongols reached us. The rodent leading them looked me square in the eyes.

"My name is **BORTE**, stranger," she said in a *haughty* squeak. "Who are you? I get the feeling I have met you before. I never forget a snout!"

She was **right**! I had already met Borte and

Genghis Khan on my last journey through time.* It was only for a moment, but she had made a big impression.

I was so **agitated** that I responded without thinking. "Yes, we've already met, very **briefly**. My name is Geronimu Khan! And this is Maya and Wild Willie . . ."

Roborat-8 pinched my ear. "**Careful**, Geronimoid! **Khan** means 'leader' . . . which means this could get **ugly**!"

Borte was already eyeing me suspiciously. "*Khan*? Are you the leader of a tribe?"

"Um, not quite . . .

KHAN

Khan is an ancient Mongol title. Originally it meant "leader," but after Genghis Khan's conquests, the term was used to describe sovereigns of the kingdoms that his empire was divided into. The title *Genghis Khan* meant "Universal Ruler." Genghis Khan's true name was Temüjin.

*Read all about it in my book *The Race Against Time*!

er, I said **Khan**, because where I'm from I — I am a leader . . ." I stammered.

She interrupted me. "Say no more, I get it! You are a Shaman — no, a head shaman!"

"Well, I'm not a shaman, either. I am a **writer** and a **traveler**!" I said.

"I see. You would be a great **ADVISOR** for my Temüjin!" Borte exclaimed.

A tall rodent stepped forward, scowling. He had **bushy** black eyebrows and two dark eyes that shot me a look as sharp as a cheese knife. He was wearing a **wolf tooth** necklace, which clinked when he moved.

He **circled** me, looking me up and down from my whiskers to my tail. It was a look of jealousy . . . no, hostility . . . no, **WICKEDNESS**!

He turned to Borte. "You want this little rat here to be an advisor? With that *silly* snout?" he grumbled. "Tell me now, what do **YOU** know how to do?" he demanded.

"Silence, Malefian Khan!" Borte snapped.

But he turned his back to me and thundered, "Only I am the *shaman* of this tribe and the leader of all the Mongol shamans. Only I shall be the personal advisor to Genghis Khan! Mouse from faraway lands, do you see this **wolf tooth** necklace? It was given to me by the Great Khan himself, with his own paws!" Then he lowered his squeak and hissed, "You'll Never take my place, rat! I won't let you!"

You won't take my place, rat!

I WILL BE LOYAL, GREAT KHAN!

I was going to answer that I had *no intention* of taking his spot as advisor, nor as shaman, since I wasn't a shaman! But Borte ended the conversation by striding away, signaling for us to **follow her**. She headed toward an encampment of round tents on the steppe.

The setting sun lit up the patches of **snow** beginning to melt. Spring was right around the corner!

"Those are **gers**, Geronimoid!" Roborat-8 whispered in my ear. "They are the typical tents of the nomadic tribes on the steppe . . ." Then he began to bombard me with *INFORMATION*. "Listen up, Geronimoid, and you might learn something! You need this information! **Good thing** I'm here to educate you . . ."

The *Ger*

A *ger*, or yurt, is a traditional, tentlike Mongol dwelling with a structure that was easy to take apart and put back together. It was erected with wooden poles, which were then covered with skins or thick cloths. When it was time for the Mongols to change grazing locations, they would load up the *gers* on carts and move them.

A *ger* was supported by *khana*, a series of circular wooden frames. The roof was made of a *tono* (dome) and *uni* (long wooden beams). It was supported in the center by two poles, called *bagana*. The entire *ger* was covered in felt made of wool from goats, yaks, or sheep.

The *khalga* (door) was made of decorated wood, and it always pointed southward.

The areas inside the *ger* had specific meanings: the spot of honor was positioned to the north. The west side was for the men, and the east side was for the women. In the center was the stove, the center of family life.

I'm here to educate!

How do I turn you off?!

Once more, I regretted the fact that Roborat-8 didn't have an **OFF** switch to power him down. He was yammering on and on, and I was sure **Borte** would hear him. Desperate, I whispered, "That's absolutely fascinating. But now, please, **be quiet**!"

I was on the verge of **EXPLODING** with impatience when Roborat-8 abruptly fell silent. We had arrived in front of a *ger* that was larger than the others.

Borte opened the **ornate**, brightly colored door and entered. We followed her inside, where a mouse was seated on a sort of couch in the northernmost part of the *ger*. It was he:

**the great,
the mythical,
the powerful,
the invincible . . .
Genghis Khan!**

Circular enclosure (*khana*)

Carpets

Table for serving food and tea

Pillows

We waited in silence while all types of rodents — young mice and old, males and females, soldiers and generals — passed before **Genghis Khan**, turning to him for advice, protection, and justice.

I admired the patience with which he listened to everyone, as well as the wisdom with which he responded. He was truly a **great leader**, and not just because of his abilities in combat!

When the last of his subjects had passed before him, Borte squeaked in his ear. I could only make out a few words: "Pssst . . . shaman . . . writer . . . advisor . . . What do you say, Temüjin?"

The Great Khan reflected at length. He **STARED** at me with an intense gaze. Then he stroked his long whiskers. "Approach, mouse!" he said. "You say you are a writer and a traveler, yet when my wife and I met you the first time you disappeared suddenly.* How did you do that?"

---

*In *The Race Against Time*, I fled suddenly from Genghis Khan in the Paw Pro Portal.

I bowed so low my whiskers hit the ground.

"Great Genghis, this must remain my **SECRET**. I cannot reveal it to you," I answered.

Genghis exchanged a knowing glance with Borte. "I understand and respect your secret. But are you ready to swear your **loyalty** to me? Know that I tolerate neither betrayal nor lies!"

"I will be loyal, **Great Khan**!" I exclaimed.

At that point, Wild Willie squeaked up. "Great Khan, we are Wild Willie and Maya. We accompany Geronimu on his journey, and we will also be **LOYAL** to you!"

I will be loyal!

You're Getting Sleepy . . . Very, Very Sleeeeeepy . . .

Genghis Khan nodded in satisfaction. "Mongols, here are two new **fighters** and here is Geronimu Khan! I name him my personal advisor, like Malefian."

"Long live Geronimu Khan!" everyone cried.

Everyone, that is, but Malefian. "'Long live'?" he hissed. "Not if I have anything to say about it. May he **drop dead** right now!" He shot me a **FIERY** look. "I challenge you, Geronimu!"

"You disappoint me, Malefian," said

Zap!

152

the Great Khan, sighing. "I hoped you would collaborate with him, but if you want to challenge him . . . let the duel begin!"

Greasy cat guts, I was in **TROUBLE**! I pretended to scratch my snout and **FLICKED** Roborat-8, who was hiding under my hat. "Now you decide to be quiet? Come on, say something! Give me an **idea**, or this time it's 'good-bye, world' for sure!"

"Ah, so now you want me to talk?" the little robot muttered. "**How convenient!** First you tell me to shut my snout, then you tell me to talk, or else. Make up your mind!"

I groaned. "Talk as much as you want to, okay? Just get me out of this mess!"

Roborat-8 chuckled. "*HEE, HEE, HEE!* Perfect! From now on, I'll chatter like a chipmunk. And you can't stop me!"

I didn't have time to respond. Malefian was removing his wolf tooth pendant from his neck

You are sleeeepppyyy · · ·

and **Swinging** it before my eyes.

"Look me in the eyes . . . Geeeeronimu Khaaaaan, you're getting **sleepy, sleeepy** . . . veeeeery **sleeeepy** . . ." he said.

A deep tiredness was slowly coming over me. I murmured, "Yes, I'm **sleepy** · · · **sleeeepy** · · · **sleeepy** . . . **so sleeeeeeepy** . . ."

ZZZZZ zzzzz **ZZZZZ** zzzzz
ZZZZZ **ZZZZZ** zzzzz **ZZZZZ**
ZZZZZ zzzzz **zzzzz** zzzzz
zzzzz **ZZZZZ** **zzzzz** **ZZZZZ**

I was just falling totally asleep, when I felt a sharp **pinch** on

my ear. It was Roborat-8. "Wake up, Geronimoid! What are you doing, falling asleep in the middle of a **duel**? Come on, we'll use this!"

He pulled a superpowerful **laser** from one of his secret compartments. Then he lifted the edges of my hat and pointed a ray of **BLINDING** light right at Malefian!

"*Ooohhhhhhhhhh!*" the crowd cried.

The shaman stumbled. "**Squeak!** I must admit, you're good, rat," he yelled. "But this isn't over!"

He turned away from me for a moment and then turned back with a **TERRIFYING** mask over his snout. It scared the cheese out of me!

I **JUMPED**, about to faint from fright.

But Roborat-8 was ready. He **sprayed** a stream of freezing water at Malefian. "Let me take care of him!" he cried. And with that, he projected a hologram of a **T. rex** — a giant dinosaur — right in front of us!

Eeeek!

Aaaaaaah!

Everyone began to scream. "**HELP!** Have mercy!"

"How did he do that?"

"Geronimu is really powerful!"

"He made a giant **monster** appear! It looks like a dragon! What is it?"*

Malefian turned WHITER than the steppe after a new snow. He stayed in place, fixing his lightning gaze at me. Then he pulled a handful of

Grrr . . .

*The Mongol people didn't know about the existence of prehistoric animals.

dust out of his shoulder bag and threw it into the fireplace.

A cloud of SMELLY green smoke rose from the fire.

From under my fur hat, Roborat-8 snorted. "What a cheap trick! Okay, Geronimoid, do as I say. On the count of three, **step away** from Malefian, got it?"

Then he whispered, "One, two . . . three!"

I jumped far from Malefian as Roborat-8 shot a MULTICOLORED laser at him. It singed the shaman's whiskers!

One, two . . . three!

Aaaargh!

WELL DONE?
WHO, ME?!

All the Mongols snickered. "**Ha, ha, ha!**
Geronimu scorched the shaman's whiskers!"

Now Malefian was **MADDER** than a cat
with a bad case of fleas. He grabbed a huge **club**
and began chasing after me, yelling, "I'll teach you
to challenge the only true shaman and advisor to
Genghis Khan! Since none of my **tricks** have

I'll mash
you up, rat!

Bonk!

worked yet, you leave me no choice. I will use an old tried-and-true method! I will **mash** you like millet! I will **snap** your little bones like toothpicks! I will line my boots with your fur — that way I'll crush you with every step I take!"

"**HEEEEEEELP!**" I yelled.

All the Mongols were bent over with **LAUGHTER**. "Look at those two **FIGHTING** like cats and rats! Let's see who will win!"

Get back here!

Heeeeeelp!

"Come on, you can do it, Geronimo!" Maya urged me.

"Rookie, fight like a **REAL MOUSE**! Use those muscles!" Wild Willie shouted.

Malefian was about to grab me, when Genghis Khan got to his paws. "**STOP**, Malefian, this isn't right!" he thundered in outrage. "I will not allow you to commit this **INJUSTICE** in front of me, and in my *ger*, no less! A true shaman doesn't have to attack using force. Your behavior shows that you are not a trustworthy advisor!"

When he heard the Great Khan squeak, Malefian stopped short. He took off the **WOLF TOOTH** necklace, the symbol of his position, and pawed it to me.

"Here, rat. This is yours now. But I will get my revenge — oh, I will get my revenge!"

Cold **sweat** began to drip from my whiskers. Without meaning to, I had made a terrible enemy!

"Mongols, honor Geronimu, Genghis Khan's new advisor!" Borte shouted.

I **bowed** down until my whiskers grazed the ground. "Thank you. This is such an **HONOR**!"

Maya **patted** me on the back (which almost made me topple over). "**WELL DONE!** You did a pretty good job in that duel!" she said.

"Well done? Who, m-me?!" I stammered. "You're welcome — I mean, thanks! Honestly, it was pure **LUCK** . . ." ☘

"Tell the truth, Geronimoid, it was all thanks to

Well done!

Umm . . . th-thanks . . .

me! If it hadn't been for me, you'd be **CAT CHOW** by now!" Roborat-8 yelled.

My fur turned redder than a tomato. Fortunately, everyone's attention was on **Genghis Khan**. "Now that the wicked shaman has gone and peace has returned, everyone must return to his or her own *ger*," he proclaimed. "We need to complete our arrangements for *Tsagaan Sar*, *the Feast of the White Moon*, which we will celebrate tomorrow!"

Wild Willie, Maya, and I headed toward the **EXIT** of Genghis Khan's tent like everyone else. Then a gentle paw touched my tail.

It was Borte. "Geronimu, it's **dark** out now. You and

TSAGAAN SAR
Tsagaan Sar is the feast of the Lunar New Year, marking the arrival of spring. The night before *Tsagaan Sar* is a moonless night, called *Bituun*, and then the new moon rises on the first day of the new year. On the eve of *Tsagaan Sar*, the Mongols wait for it by eating to their hearts' content. They believe that if they are hungry on this day, they will be hungry all year!

your friends should stay for dinner! The night before the feast is called *Bituun*, the moonless night, and it is the custom of our clan to spend it feasting in the

WHITE FOOD
Tsagaan Sar is also the feast of the white food. To celebrate, the Mongols eat light-colored food, such as rice, milk, cheese, and *buuz*, which are steamed dumplings with goat or sheep meat.

company of others. It brings **good luck** for the New Year!"

We thanked our host for the INVITATION and made ourselves comfortable at the center of the *ger* along with Borte, Genghis Khan, and their children, Jochi, Ögedei, Chagatai, and Tolui. There were many white CANDLES burning in the tent, and soon the scrumptious scent of tasty food filled the air.

buuz

Borte served us **delicious** dishes: *buuz*, steamed dumplings filled with

cheeses

mutton; rice; and then cheese — cheese after cheese! **YUM!**

"Do you smell that?" Genghis Khan said proudly. "They say that the smell of food keeps all the **EVIL SPIRITS** far from your home!"

He turned and gave Borte a look of pride. "Borte, you are an **EXCEPTIONAL WIFE.** You are my best friend and my most valued advisor, and you are also an **amazing** cook!"

Then he turned to us. "I have known Borte since we were **children** . . . I fought my first battle for her . . ."

Then he began to tell us the story of his life. I couldn't resist — I pulled out a **notebook** and a pen. "Great Khan, may I write? I would love to tell the **STORY** of your life one day!"

He **smiled**, pleased. "Write, write, Geronimu!" Then he began squeaking.

I started taking notes, but soon, I stopped. "Hey,

I am from the barbaric north. I wear the same clothing and eat the same food as the cowherds and horse-herders. We make the same sacrifices and we share our riches.

I look upon the nation as a newborn child, and I care for my soldiers as though they were my brothers . . .

When it was wet, we bore the wet together, when it was cold, we bore the cold together.

No friend is better than your own wise heart! Although there are many things you can rely on, no one is more reliable than yourself.

All these words were said to be actually spoken by Genghis Khan!

wait a sec . . . *When* was Genghis born?"

"Geronimoid, you are such a **cheesebrain** sometimes," muttered Roborat-8. "He was born in 1162! The **MONGOL CALENDAR** is different than ours because it's based on the cycle of the **moon**. Oh, it's a good thing I'm here to explain it all to you!"

When Genghis Khan finished his story, Wild Willie and Maya began to squeak with him about **BATTLES**, strategies, and combat techniques.

The Great Khan was impressed by their **interest** in and **KNOWLEDGE** of warfare. He decided to put them in charge of a group of a hundred warriors.

Meanwhile, I was **writing** feverishly, trying to put all the notes I had taken in order. Borte was gazing at her husband **tenderly**, and Roborat-8 was **SNOOZING** in his perch under my fur hat. I could hear him snoring. **Zzzzzz!**

It was truly an unforgettable evening!

It was close to midnight when we thanked Genghis Khan and Borte for the great honor and headed toward the only free *ger* in the village: the one that belonged to **MALEFIAN**.

As we left, I saw Borte head toward the **LIVESTOCK** tent and leave three pieces of ice at the entrance. This was part of the tradition on that special night as well.

BITUUN, THE DARKEST NIGHT

That night, everyone in the tribe slept peacefully. I was the only one TOSSING and turning restlessly in my bed.

Malefian's tent seemed gloomy and oppressive. It was full of EERIE masks, herbs swaying in the breeze, and all kinds of spooky amulets. This *ger* had always belonged to the tribe shaman!

Lying in that STRANGE tent, full of STRANGE objects, on that STRANGE moonless night, I felt a horrible homesickness.

After an hour or so, I gave up on sleep and scurried out of the *ger*. Under that enormouse, starry sky, I felt terribly alone.

For me, it really was *Bituun,* the darkest night! Thousands of DOUBTS raced through my mind. Would we be able to find Professor von Volt? Would I ever return home and hug my dear nephew Benjamin again?

A lonely **tear** slid down my snout. I pulled out Benjamin's picture and gazed at it.

Roborat-8 slipped out of the *ger* and stood next to me. He extended his **mechanical** arm and pawed me a **TISSUE**. That mass of microcircuits really understood my **feelings**!

"Oh how I wish my nephew **Benjamin** were

Sob!

here!" I said, sighing. "He always knows how to find the fun in any situation . . ."

"That's so **sweet**," said Roborat-8. "Would you like to see your nephew?"

"Of course!" I cried. "But it's impossible. He is so far away,

171

both in space and time."

"Can I see his photo?" Roborat-8 asked.

"Of course. There, that's Benjamin!" I responded, passing him the **PHOTO**.

Before I could squeak another word, he'd grabbed it and stuck it in one of his little **DRAWERS**. Immediately, the photo got sucked in with a scary **NOISE** that sounded like a cross between a vacuum cleaner and a garbage disposal.

"Hey, give me back my photo!" I cried. "That's important to me!"

Roborat-8 giggled. "Just wait, Geronimoid! *HEE, HEE, HEE!*"

Then a strange green **FOG** began to form around me . . . "Wh-what's happening?" I stammered. "What are you d-d-doing?"

"Stop clucking like a chicken, mouse!" said Roborat-8. "It's a *SURPRISE*!"

Out of the greenish fog two bright eyes suddenly appeared . . . two sweet ears . . . and a snout that I knew well!

It was **Benjamin**! He was materializing before my eyes! Thundering cat tails, what a fabumouse **surprise**!

"Hee, hee! Do you like my **SURPRISE**?" Roborat-8 asked.

I hugged Benjamin, who by now had **MATERIALIZED** completely.

I quickly checked that his tail in the right place. **"Benjamin! Are you all right?"** I asked.

"Yes, Uncle G! I'm a bit SHAKEN up, but I'm great!" cried my nephew, hugging me. "But tell me, what's going on? Where are we? I was sleeping, when I felt a terrible **itchiness**, and then I was surrounded by a strange fog . . ."

I was about to explain, when, suddenly, a second little snout appeared out of the FOG. It had curly black fur and two rascally dark eyes.

"*Uncle G!*" a high squeak cried.

Uncle G!

Benjamin!

Wow, talk about a SURPRISE! There she was . . . Bugsy Wugsy, Benjamin's mischievous best friend!

"Holey cheese, how did I get here?" Bugsy exclaimed. "I was sleeping, when I felt something pull my fur. Then a green FOG appeared everywhere. It was so scratchy!"

"Roborat-8, what is she doing here?" I whispered.

"Hmm . . . this is **STRANGE**, truly very strange!" he said. "The long-distance dematerializer never fails, but this is the first time I've used a photo to link to the specific **space-time** coordinates for dematerialization. I must verify this at once. I hope I haven't accidentally altered anything in the rematerialization formula . . ."

After a few minutes, he spit out my **PHOTO** and held it up in satisfaction. "Ah, now I understand! Look here!"

Only then did I notice that in a **CORNER** of the photo, there was an unmistakable tuft of **curly** fur — it was Bugsy! That's why she had  rematerialized in the time of Genghis Khan, too.

Bugsy was still looking around in **confusion**.

But after a moment, she'd started chatting again.

"Hmm . . . judging by the round tents and the cold and those guards with long, droopy whiskers running this way, I would say that . . . we are in **Mongolia** during Genghis Khan's time!"

She paused for a moment. "Right? Huh? Am I right, Uncle G? Am I **GOOD** or what?"

At that moment, I realized something. Rotten rat's teeth! Now there would be **TWO** of them chattering and chatting nonstop: Roborat-8 *and* Bugsy!

Rancid ricotta, poor old me!

Soon, two of Genghis Khan's enormouse guards were asking **QUESTIONS** about where Benjamin and Bugsy had come from. They seemed very suspicious.

"Stranger, you may be Genghis Khan's new advisor and Borte's friend, but we don't like your **tricks**!" the first one thundered **threateningly**.

"We are watching you, understand?"

And they advanced toward me, swinging their swords:

ZIP! *Zing!* **SWISH!** *Zip!*

Luckily, Wild Willie and Maya arrived just in time to save me with some **secret martial arts moves**! The guards went right to sleep.

Wild Willie soon realized that two **SMALL** rodents he knew well had joined us. "Benjamin! Bugsy! What are you doing here?"

"Well, we couldn't miss this adventure!" Benjamin joked.

"Roborat-8 used our **PHOTO** to bring us here," Bugsy Wugsy explained. "Cool, right?" Then she turned to Maya. "I don't think I've met you!"

"I'm **Maya**, Wild Willie's cousin," Maya said, shaking Bugsy's paw. "I think we're going to make a great team!"

TSAGAAN SAR, THE DAY OF THE WHITE MOON

We had just curled up our tails in bed again, when a loud squeak echoed through the *ger*. "Geronimu Khan, **HURRY**, the festivities have begun!"

I jumped up. "Huh? What **festivities**? And who in the name of cheese is Geronimu?" Then I remembered that I was Geronimu Khan and that I had spent the night in a *ger*!

It was Borte's cousin who'd woken me so abruptly. "Quick, Geronimu, you're the **LAST ONE**! You need to take a **BATH**!"

"But . . . I bathed yesterday!" I protested.

"It doesn't matter! You'll do it again!"

She was relentless about making sure I had **WASHED** myself well (even behind my ears!), and then she made sure I wore the right outfit (a white *deel*). Last, she pawed me a few soft blue silk scarves. "These are for **exchanging good wishes**! You must start with the **OLDEST** rodents, whom we Mongols honor on this occasion.

> **TSAGAAN SAR AND THE COLOR WHITE**
> *Tsagaan* means "white," and the color is important to the Mongols. It is a symbol of purity and happiness. According to tradition, offering or wearing something white during the festival will ensure a successful new year.

"Remember to **grab** the paws of the elderly at the elbow, just like I'm doing," she continued. "And make sure you use the right **GREETING**

Aack!

Mmmm . . .

with everyone. '*Daaga dalantai byaruu bulchintai, sureg mal targan orov uu?*' means 'How are your animals? How did they manage the winter? Are they fat enough?' But if you turn to an elderly rodent, you must **greet them** with the special greeting for elders: '*Amar baina uu?*'"

I listened carefully and wrote down the phrases to MEMORIZE them. She made me repeat them a dozen times, to be sure I pronounced them correctly.

The entire tribe had begun preparing for the feast. Some were **bathing**, some were already lighting the first **fire** of the year, and some were leaving to go **PRAY** on the sacred mountain. Some were visiting the *ger* of relatives and friends for the traditional greeting **ceremony**.

I decided it was time to try to find out where Professor von Volt was, and scurried over to Wild Willie, Maya, Benjamin, and Bugsy.

A Surprise Attack!

When I reached my friends, I hastily explained my plan. "We need to visit ALL the tents in the encampment, starting with the eldest rodents, and ask for NEWS of the professor!"

"Good idea, rookie!" Wild Willie approved. "This is the first time I've ever heard you propose a **SENSIBLE** plan."

I like it, rookie!

Maya smiled at me. "Yes, I agree. This is the second time since we began our trip that you have **failed to disappoint** me!"

I didn't know whether to consider that a **compliment** or not, but it was the nicest thing Maya had ever said to me. Naturally, I turned as red as **tomato sauce** on cheese pizza.

Bugsy noticed right away. "Uncle G, you're bright red! I think you have a crush on Ma —"

I quickly **covered** her snout. "I don't have a crush on anyone, got it?!" I whispered in her ear.

"Calm down, Uncle G, I won't tell anyone *who* you have a **CRUSH** on," she replied. "I don't have to! It's totally obvious you have a crush on Ma —"

Luckily, Benjamin came to my rescue. "What are you two squeaking about? We need a **PICTURE** of the professor to show everyone to see if anyone's seen him."

"Do you have a **P H O T O** of professor von Volt in your memory?" I asked Roborat-8.

"No, I don't have any pictures of the professor," he said regretfully. "He doesn't like being photographed, otherwise I would have rematerialized him right away and we would never have had to leave on this journey."

"Bugsy and I can take care of it," Benjamin said. "We are the best ARTISTS in our class. We'll try to sketch the professor . . ."

He immediately took a piece of birch BARK and a **burnt** stick and got to work. After a few minutes, he and Bugsy proudly showed us their work . . .

Well, Roborat-8 definitely wouldn't have been able to rematerialize Professor von Volt with Benjamin and Bugsy's sketch. But the picture was a good enough likeness that at least we could show the image to the mice of the village and see if our friend had passed through.

I put the drawing in my sack, and we began our **SEARCH**. We spent all day visiting *gers*, chatting and eating delicious traditional plates. We tried *buuz* and many WHITE foods like yogurt and cheese — my favorite!

We showed everyone the sketch, but unfortunately we found **no trace** of the professor. No one seemed to have seen him!

Only toward the end of the day did an older rodent have good news for us. She said the sketch looked like a **MeRCHaNt** who had come to barter his wares a few days earlier.

Was the mouse she'd seen Professor von Volt?

Cheesecake! It was hard to say . . .

The Mongols were very kind to us, but at the end of the day, we were *DRAINED*, discouraged, and our tummies were very full. BUUURp!

We dragged ourselves to our *ger*. I changed my clothes, and we fell sound asleep!

ZZZZZZZZZZZZZZZZZ...
ZZZZZZ...
ZZZZZZZZZZZZZZZ...
ZZZZZZZZZZZZZZZZZ...

A little while later, I woke up feeling restless. The whole village was in a **DEEP SLEEP**, but there was a **strange silence** on the steppe.

I stole out of the tent and went to see Genghis Khan, Borte, and the Mongol generals. They were still awake, studying a **map** drawn on leather.

"Come, Geronimu, give us your advice," Borte called to me. "Today a messenger came to warn us of an **enemy** horde marching toward our village."

"Oh no! When will they attack?" I asked.

Genghis Khan showed me the map. "It depends. If the enemies took the *safest* route, they will be here in a week. If they take the **shortest** route, they will be here in two days . . ."

I pointed to another road that was barely **sketched** on the map. "And if they took this third route?"

Genghis shook his snout. "That's **impossible**. We are the only ones who know of it."

Just then a terrible scream tore through the night, followed by a tremendous wailing. It was the **BATTLE** cry of the enemy! They were swooping down on the defenseless village like a pack of hungry cats on a herd of sleeping mouselings.

"Betrayal!" Genghis Khan shouted. "Someone has revealed our SECRET ROUTE to our enemies!"

The Great Khan and his generals darted out of the tent, drawing their **SWORDS**. In a flash, Wild Willie and Maya joined them. Soon, they were boldly fighting side by side.

Genghis's warriors were sleepy and unprepared to face the ***attack***. They grabbed their weapons to try to defend their families. But the **disadvantages** of being taken by surprise were too great to be overcome by courage alone.

I quickly reached Benjamin and Bugsy, ready to **DEFEND THEM** with my life. It was then that

I discovered who had betrayed the rodents of the village.

There, lined up in the enemy's front lines, right next to the enemy general, was the **evil** Malefian!

As soon as he saw me, Malefian cackled. "The time has come for **revenge**, Geronimu! I will slice up your whiskers and mangle your tail. I will turn you into mouse meatballs!"

I needed an attack plan, and fast! But I was too **TERRIFIED**. I couldn't think straight! I began scrambling through the encampment, and Malefian **FOLLOWED ME** on horseback.

I **SCURRIED** to avoid his blows. I could feel his sharp blade brush past my tail. **Swish!**

I closed my eyes, waiting for the blow that would take off my tail forever, and yelled desperately,

"SQUEEEAAAK!"

DISCO EFFECT, ACTIVATE!

Just when I thought all was lost, something unexpected happened. *ROBORAT-8* jumped out from behind a chest he'd been using as a hiding spot and shouted:

"MUSIC, ACTIVATE! DISCO EFFECT, ACTIVATE!"

Suddenly, a wild dance party began! Roborat-8's drawers began projecting streams of **COLORED** light in the sky, and loud music **BLASTED**.

I recognized the tune right away. It was the latest hit from the most popular rock group in New Mouse City, the **Rolling Cheese**, Benjamin and Bugsy's **favorite** band. The effect was so deafening that the enemy troops immediately retreated in confusion. They were **terrified** by the piercing shrieks of the lead singer.

When the drum solo began, the enemies really hustled. The song's loud bass line made them think we were much **stronger** than they were! It sounded like the pounding of millions of paws. The enemy even left the cart with all their booty on the battlefield.

"Victory! The enemy is fleeing!" Genghis Khan's troops cried.

I hugged Benjamin, Bugsy, and Roborat-8. It was thanks to them that I wasn't mousemeat! The three of them exchanged high fives, and cheered, "WE DID IT! WE ARE SO TOUGH!"

The three of them had become fast friends. It warmed my heart!

Genghis Khan congratulated us. "May you have long lives, warriors! But tell me, where did you learn such a **TERRIFYING** combat technique?"

"Umm . . . actually, in our land that isn't a combat technique," I responded, a bit

embarrassed. "Our mouselings adore it. They think it's music."

He shook his snout. "I respect the customs of other rodents, but I must say, your music is totally BARBARIC!"

I burst out laughing. "I agree, Great Khan, it is the kind of music that bursts your eardrums and pierces your brain. When I hear it, I feel like your enemies: It makes me want to RUN AWAY!"

Genghis Khan laughed. "Well, thank you, friends. It is because of you we are still ALIVE! You must receive your share of the bounty."

I bowed until my whiskers grazed the ground. "Great Genghis, I appreciate your generosity, but I prefer not to accept my share of the spoils. I will DONATE it to those who are more needy than I."

My friends agreed. "Thank you, Great Khan, but we don't need it, either."

Genghis Khan nodded, pleased. Then he gave the order to divvy up the **SPOILS**. Everyone in his group got a part of the bounty.

Among the furs, shields, lances, clothes, and jewels, a small, ENGRAVED wooden chest stood out. It held the jewels of the wife of the enemy leader. Genghis Khan wanted only that small **chest** to offer as a gift to Borte.

"This is for you, my courageous wife!" he said.

Borte opened it with a **swift flick** of her sword. Soon she was pulling out shell necklaces, silver **jewelry**, and . . . a precious mirror!

I recognized it immediately. It was CLEOPATRA'S MIRROR!

"What is this?" Borte asked, curious.

"It is a **most precious** mirror," I responded. "It comes from ancient Egypt and belonged to Cleopatra, a great queen."

"I have never seen such a finely decorated mirror," Borte exclaimed. "What a strange coincidence . . . Just a few days ago, a traveling merchant passed through our **VILLAGE** and asked if I had a mirror with a precious handle. That rodent had a strange accent and an ODD way of behaving, just like you. And just like you he wore a strange, clear **butterfly*** on his nose . . ."

*Borte is talking about Geronimo's glasses. The Mongols didn't know what they were.

I slapped myself on the snout. That was surely Professor von Volt! He had reached the village too **early**, before the mirror reached Borte. Then maybe he'd tried to find it with Genghis Khan's enemies, but hadn't reached them in time, either.

Who knew **WHERE** — or **WHEN** — the professor was now? Probably in the time of Dante and Beatrice in Florence, Italy, in 1283. Beatrice Portinari was the third mouselet to possess this PRECIOUS object!

Good-bye!

I winked at my friends and beckoned them. It was **time to go**!

We let the Mongols know that we needed to leave. Borte turned to me. "You're leaving so suddenly, Geronimu. But you will RETURN, right?" Her squeak was full of feeling.

"Who knows?" I replied. "Maybe one day we will see each other again! **GOOD-BYE**, Borte! **GOOD-BYE**, Genghis Khan! It was lovely seeing you again!"

Then my friends and I scampered away. We reached a hidden clearing, where we returned the *TAIL TRANSPORTER* to its regular size.

As soon as we were onboard, Roborat-8 punched in the coordinates for the next stop: *Florence, 1283!*

With a loud *bang*, the Rat-o-Ray started up again . . . and again I felt itchy all over. We were dematerializing!

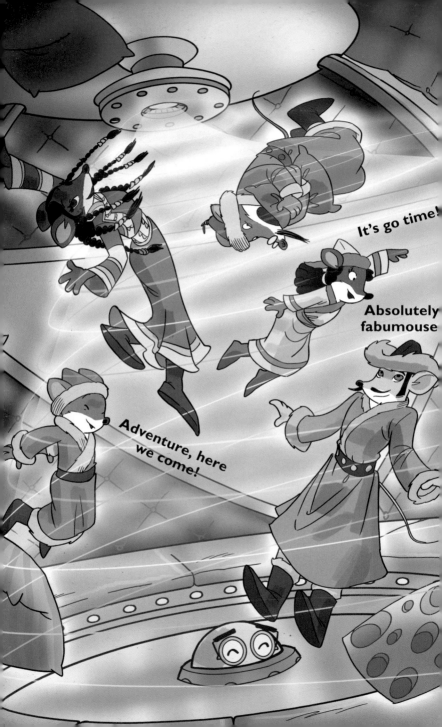

Fashion in Dante and Beatrice's Time

Moldy mozzarella, check out the refined fashions of the medieval rodents!

Long, lavish clothes that were richly decorated with embroidery — now *that* was high fashion! Plus, cloaks, doublets, velvet tunics . . . how stylish!

I feel like a true squire!

The Middle Ages are so fascinating!

Do I look like a noble lady?

SHOES: Shoes in the Middle Ages were long and pointy. Some were so pointy that they were double the length of the foot of the person wearing them!

HATS: Bonnets, caps, hats . . . in the Middle Ages, hats were truly a fashion essential.

CLOAKS: Both men and women wore cloaks, often with a hood.

BAGS: Bags of all shapes completed both women's and men's outfits. They could be made of fabric or leather.

Our clothes are super comfortable!

LIZARD GREEN, APPLE GREEN . . . OR *VOMIT* GREEN?

The golden sphere rematerialized us a few moments later.

I felt the usual **itching** all over my fur, but I was starting to get used to it. Just to be certain, I checked that my nose, tail, and ears were in the **right** place . . . you never know!

Benjamin and Bugsy giggled.

"What a funny feeling! That was better than a ride at an amousement park!" Bugsy said.

"Yeah, it was just like a trip to Ratty Potter World!" Benjamin agreed.

Maya and Wild Willie were **UNDISTURBED**, as always. I, on the other paw, felt a wave of **nausea**, reminding me of being on a boat.

The Tail Transporter was swaying gently back and forth. Yes, it was just like being seasick! And I can assure you that I know quite a bit about **seasickness**!

Maya looked at me for a moment. "Geronimo, you know you're turning a **LIZARD GREEN** color?"

"No, no, I think it's more of an **apple green**," Wild Willie argued.

Then Roborat-8 butted in. "No, no, no, it's **vomit green**! Hee, hee, hee!"

As the three of them discussed the exact **SHADE** of my fur, I threw open the door of the Tail Transporter and looked outside.

My **EYES** opened wider than a wheel of Gouda. Cheese niblets, I was right to be seasick . . . or should I say, **RIVER-SICK**!

The Tail Transporter was floating along a river

running through the lush countryside.

Roborat-8 peeked out behind me and scanned the landscape. "By triangulating, taking into consideration the debris accumulation and the **rotation** of the earth, then subtracting my birthday and cubing the length of Professor von Volt's tail, plus the size of Dewey's shoes . . . I can say definitively that this river is, without a doubt, the **Arno**! We have arrived!"

"I don't care if it's the Arno or the Amazon, **just get me out of it**!" I cried.

I began to row with my **paws**. A few minutes later, the current had washed us onto a **ROCKY** little beach.

I sprawled on the ground as my friends jumped out eagerly.

After a minute or two, Maya **fanned** me with a leaf. "Poor Geronimo, you're so weak . . . you have to be **delicate** to suffer from river-sickness!"

I was thrilled she was taking care of me, but I was ashamed to look like such a weakling. So I scrambled unsteadily to my paws.

"Oh, I'm better already . . . It must've been that huge mountain of cheese I ate yesterday."

Luckily, everyone was busy reshaping their clothes into medieval styles, and no one noticed I'd turned redder than a boiled lobster. Would my embarrassment never end?

When we were ready, we scurried along the riverbank. Soon we reached a road.

I looked around. "How lucky for us — a wagon is coming!" I cried.

What a terrible stench!

But a few seconds later, the wind brought a dreadful **smell** our way. "What a stench! It's a wagon filled with **manure**!" I exclaimed, disappointed.

But I plugged my nose and asked the driver, "Exguse me, bwhat's the best bway to bet to Flborence?"

The rodent driving the **wagon** looked at me, confused. "Oh, hello, stranger! You must be coming from very far away if you don't know where Florence is! Either that, or you're

What a cheesebrain!

Exguse me . . .

a bunch of **cheesebrains** . . ."

Then he looked me over from paw to snout. "Yup, cheesebrains it is! But actually, we — my mule and I — are going to **Florence**. Do you want a lift?"

I *really* didn't want to get on a wagon filled with manure! But Wild Willie exclaimed, "**Thanks a lot!**" He and Maya jumped on the mule, Benjamin and Bugsy sat next to the driver, and I was forced to climb in the back, right into the stinky **manure**! Ugh! Roborat-8 perched on my head.

And that's how we traveled, with that **terrible stench**, until dawn the next day, when we finally reached Florence.

As soon as I got off the wagon, I jumped into a big fountain to get the stink out of my fur.

"How will we find Beatrice, Dante's beloved?" I asked, **worried**. "Professor von Volt must be

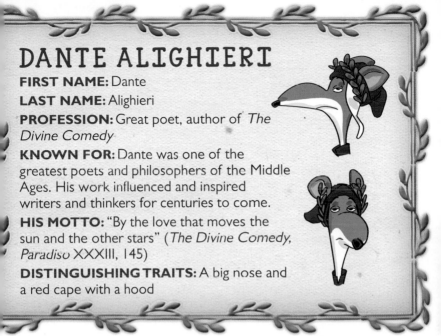

DANTE ALIGHIERI

FIRST NAME: Dante

LAST NAME: Alighieri

PROFESSION: Great poet, author of *The Divine Comedy*

KNOWN FOR: Dante was one of the greatest poets and philosophers of the Middle Ages. His work influenced and inspired writers and thinkers for centuries to come.

HIS MOTTO: "By the love that moves the sun and the other stars" (*The Divine Comedy, Paradiso* XXXIII, 145)

DISTINGUISHING TRAITS: A big nose and a red cape with a hood

looking for her to make sure she has Cleopatra's mirror."

Roborat-8 giggled. Then he projected a **THREE-DIMENSIONAL** image of Dante in front of us.

"Silly mouse. In 1283, Florence was a pretty small town. Finding the poet Dante will be as easy as cheddar pie! We'll recognize him by his **red cape**. And if we find him, we'll find her!"

We searched Florence all morning. Around midday, Maya had an idea. "Let's go to the **top** of a tower. We'll see better from above."

CUPID'S ARROWS

After **admiring** the city from above, we **CLIMBED DOWN** the tower stairs to continue looking for Dante.

In the market square, we spotted a rodent dressed in white and, behind her, a mouse dressed in **red**. It was the great poet Dante and his beloved, BEATRICE!

We immediately made our way through the crowd to get close to them. Meanwhile, we tried to think of an excuse to squeak with Dante.

Wild Willie had an idea. "Let's send Geronimo! As scholars and writers, they will understand each other!"

"Actually, Dante is a GREAT POET," I protested. "I am just a journalist who —"

But Maya had already agreed. "Great! Let's

introduce him as an EXPERT in something."

Roborat-8 snickered. "Yes, yes, yes; Geronimo would be a perfect

> **CUPID**
>
> In Roman mythology, Cupid is a god who is often depicted as a young winged boy. He has a bow and arrow, and is able to make anyone his arrows hit fall in love.

LOVE ADVISOR! He knows all about crushes and broken hearts."

"We could be a band of traveling performers called **CUPID'S ARROWS**!" Benjamin put in.

Immediately, Roborat-8 began pulling a flute, tambourine, and other instruments out of his drawers. "I will CAMOUFLAGE myself as a lute.* Don't worry if you don't know how to play. I'll worry about the music — you just fake it!"

Wild Willie pushed me forward, and I bumped into Dante, who was SPYING on his beloved Beatrice from behind a column.

"What a way to act, sir!" Dante exclaimed.

"Umm, excuse me, sir . . ." I mumbled. "My

---

*The lute is a stringed instrument that was popular in the Middle Ages.

name is *Geronimuccio Stiltonio*. I noticed that you are following Lady Beatrice. Are you perhaps looking to make her acquaintance?"

The great poet blushed to the roots of his fur. "Oh . . . you have discovered my **secret**, sir," he admitted. "You are very astute!"

"Well, that is my — I mean, *our* job. We are the Cupid's Arrows — a group of **singers** and **musicians** who specialize in sonnets, serenades, **love** strategies, and letters!" I explained.

I began introducing my friends. "Williardone is the lute player. Lady Maya plays the flute. And Benjamino and Bugsina play the tambourine, and can also deliver your *love letters*. And I, umm . . . I sing! If you'd like, we can help you write a love letter that will **MELT** even the coldest of hearts."

Dante's snout lit up with hope.

"Oooh . . . you are the mice for me! When can you get to work?"

"Right away, Dante, sir!"

He sighed. "I'm desperate: I just can't start a conversation with Lady Beatrice! When I see her, my tongue STICKS to the roof of my mouth, I turn RED, my heart beats like crazy, and . . ."

Maya put her paw on his shoulder. "I understand, friend: You have the classic symptoms of someone who is *hopelessly in love!*"

"She's right, and I would know," I said. I began to explain to him the **ten stages of love**, and typical symptoms of each.

Dante stared at me in **admiration**. "My compliments, sir, you are a true expert!"

At that moment, Beatrice passed in front of us. She was walking through the streets of the city with her snout high and a **dreamy** air about her. She was dressed in gray and had braided blond fur. She seemed to be **floating** two feet off the ground.

Her sweet expression gave the impression that she had a sweet heart.

Dante gazed at her for a moment, and then . . . *fainted*!

Wild Willie grabbed him before he could bonk his snout on the ground. "Sir Dante, you are really a *desperate* case!"

THE TEN STAGES OF LOVE

Dante took us to his **STUDY**, where he wrote his poetry. The room's walls were lined with shelves packed with **books**. He proudly showed us some illuminated manuscripts, including a valuable edition of Virgil's *Aeneid*. I was **WONDERSTRUCK** with admiration.

"Ahh, Virgil, what a sublime poet . . ." Dante sighed. "I consider him my greatest *teacher*."

As Dante and I began to compose a **love** poem, the others went beneath Beatrice's balcony to practice their serenade.

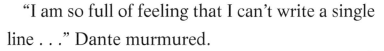

"I am so full of feeling that I can't write a single line . . ." Dante murmured.

"Don't worry! You just have a bit of *writer's block*," I reassured him. "I'll help you! Let's see. What would you like to praise about your beloved?"

He reflected. "Well, she's **kind** and honest, and her **VIRTUE** enchants everyone who meets her."

I smiled. "Great, so write exactly that! Have faith in yourself, and you will see, you'll write marvemouse love sonnets that will be remembered for centuries to come!"

Comforted by my advice, he began to write:

So gentle and virtuous she appears,

My lady, when greeting other people

That every tongue tremblingly grows silent,

And eyes do not dare gaze upon her . . . *

*This famous sonnet is part of Dante Alighieri's "Vita Nuova." It was written in homage to Beatrice. With these poetic verses, Dante says that his lady, Beatrice, is so gentle and so honest that all who see her are so struck by her sweetness that they go quiet and feel love spread throughout their own hearts.

We worked for hours and hours as my friends practiced their serenade. Finally, we were ready for our **mission**.

Dante urged us on. "Quick, let's go to Beatrice's balcony!"

We arrived at **sunset**. "You see, Sir Dante, this moment is opportune. The sky is already painted **red**, the color of love," I said.

Dante was full of feeling. But right at that moment, **other suitors** arrived, each one accompanied by a group of musicians.

"Don't fear, Sir Dante, I'll get rid of the competition!" Wild Willie exclaimed. He burst into the group of musicians, thundering, "**SCRAM, ROOKIES!** We were here first and *we* will do the serenading!"

ENOUGH OF THAT RACKET!

A window flew open, but instead of the delicate damsel Dante **adored**, a maid came out and poured a bucket of **dirty water** on top of our snouts! "Enough of that racket!" she shouted. Then she slammed the window down again.

Dante began to sob. **"Oh nooo! All is lost!"**

Then the window opened again, and Beatrice looked out.

Oh noooo!

I recognized her, even though she was half **hidden** by the curtains. I squeaked up. "Mademoiselle, here is a *love sonnet* written expressly for you by Sir Dante Alighieri!"

Dante timidly stuck his snout out from a bush, stuttering, "Y-yes, i-it is I! I am **Dante Alighieri**!"

I am Dante!

Wild Willie started playing the lute, accompanied by Maya on the flute. They sounded amazing . . . until I noticed that they were actually just **PRETENDING** to play. Roborat-8 was transmitting the music through his speakers!

I began to sing, trying to follow the tempo. "*So gentle and virtuous she appeeears . . .*"

After we finished, Beatrice **smiled**. Then she shut the curtains and disappeared.

Dante was **agitated**. "Oh, dear, I wonder if

she liked the serenade? Or maybe . . . maybe she liked the **SERENADE** but she doesn't like me . . ."

Then he pulled me aside. "Tell me, Sir Geronimuccio, do you think I have a **big nose**?" he whispered in my ear.

I tried to respond in a very diplomatic way. "Sir Dante, that is not the point. You have great qualities of **spirit** and intellect, and that's what you need to count on!"

"You're serious?" he replied, looking encouraged. "And now what should I do? Tell me, since you are an expert in love . . ."

I thought for a moment. "I've got it! Tomorrow **MORNING**, I will take you to look for a nice **GIFT** for Beatrice. You will choose it from the **HEART**, and she'll be sure to love it!"

The next morning, Dante and I visited all the shops of Florence.

"We could give her a **RING** . . ." he proposed.

"No, no, no!" I objected. "That's too much — it could embarrass her."

"Then we could get her a perfume," Dante suggested.

"No, that would be like telling her she's stinkier than Gorgonzola," I demurred.

"Then how about an oil for her delicate complexion?" he suggested.

"No, no! That would imply she has wrinkles. Trust me, Sir Dante, never give a female rodent cream for her snout!" I exclaimed.

"Okay, Geronimuccio, what do you say to a nice bouquet of flowers?" he suggested.

"Hmm . . . too ordinary," I protested.

"How about a LACE handkerchief?" he suggested.

"No — that's like asking her to cry!" I squeaked.

Dante was getting **EXASPERATED**.

"So then, what do I give her?"

"We need to keep looking. We will find the perfect gift for her. Be patient!" I counseled him.

Just then, we passed by a shop with a sign that read: EXOTIC AND ANTIQUE OBJECTS.

We entered, and Dante pointed to something that was glimmering and sparkling on display. "What do you think of that? Would that work?"

I recognized it immediately. It was CLEOPATRA'S MIRROR!

Then I understood why we hadn't encountered Professor von Volt in Florence. Once more, he'd arrived **too early**, before the object landed in Beatrice's paws! He'd probably already left and was now waiting for us in the time of Queen Elizabeth I. She was the last rodent to possess the mirror!

Dante pointed to the mirror again, distracting me from my thoughts. "So what do you say?"

"It's **perfect**!" I exclaimed enthusiastically.

Dante bought the mirror. Before he could put it in a **rosewood** case, I quickly checked that Caesar's message for Cleopatra was still in the handle.

Dante paired the gift with the sonnet he'd composed for Beatrice. We entrusted the case to Benjamin and Bugsy, who **scurried** to bring it to her.

You can count on us, Uncle G!

When Dante positioned himself beneath BEATRICE'S window that evening, she finally emerged onto her balcony.

"I enjoyed your GIFT," she murmured, holding the mirror in her paw, "but I especially enjoyed your words, Sir Dante!"

At that point, Dante was so overcome that he FAINTED! Wild Willie had to carry him home.

"Beatrice . . . oh, Beatrice . . ." Dante repeated.

It was time say good-bye to him — we were in a HURRY to get to Professor von Volt.

When I gave him my paw, he leaned in close. "Sir Geronimuccio, before you go, can I ask you for another piece of advice?" he asked me under his breath. "I have a new work in mind. It's very interesting, but I don't know what I should call it."

"The Divine Comedy?" I suggested.

"Fabumouse!" he exclaimed. "That is precisely the title I was looking for! But I am missing the

words to start off with. Do you have any ideas?"

I **smiled** under my whiskers, because *The Divine Comedy* is one of my favorite works. So I recited the beginning from memory:

"Midway upon the journey of our life
I found myself within a dark forest
for the straightforward pathway had been lost..."

Dante was thrilled. "Oh, thank you, Sir Geronimuccio: You really know your way around words. It's such a **SHAME** you have to leave!"

We said **affectionate** good-byes. Then we scurried out of Dante's villa and into the night. Since it was dark, we brought the **Tail Transporter** back to its original size right in the middle of the street.

We all boarded, and Roborat-8 entered coordinates into the Rat-o-Ray for our next destination: **London in 1595**, during the reign of Elizabeth I!

BOWS, RIBBONS, FEATHERS, LACE, AND RUFF!

After a moment that seemed to last a lifetime, the bluish fog lifted. I felt the usual itchiness, a sign that I was rematerializing. As usual, I checked to make sure my tail was in the right place — you never know!

As soon as we got our bearings, we began to shape our clothing according to the English fashions of 1595, during the reign of Queen Elizabeth I.

Roborat-8 began to pull out bows, ribbons, jewels, feathers, lace, a ruff,* and powdered wigs!

Meanwhile, he was SPITTING out orders. "Make that cuff bigger, Wild Willie! Geronimo, make those breeches shorter! Make that skirt wider, Maya! No, wider!"

*A ruff is a folded, wheel-shaped collar that was worn by both men and women in Elizabethan times.

He projected images of the fashion of the time taken from **PAINTINGS**. Then he began giving us detailed instructions on court etiquette. He went on and on about bowing and curtsying, and he made us **practice** everything.

"Bend that knee more, Stilton! Bugsy, smile a little **sweeter**, and keep your eyes down!"

"Me? Eyes down?! No way!" she protested.

Finally, Roborat-8 gave us a **WARNING**. "Remember, every time someone says the word **queen**, you must put your paw over your heart and exclaim, 'Long live the Queen!'"

After putting on a corset and a skirt as **poofy** as a hot air balloon, Maya decided she'd had enough. "Ugh! I'm suffocating! I have no intention of staying imprisoned inside this . . . this *thing* . . . another second! This time, I'm disguising myself as a **gentlemouse**!"

As she was squeaking, she reshaped her clothing

English Fashion of the Late 1500s

What lavish clothing they wore in the late 1500s! During this period, English people were very elegant, but often very uncomfortable. Both men and women wore elaborate outfits decorated with brooches and clips. The typical lady's clothing consisted of a corset, a bodice, a ruff, and a wide hoop skirt. The men wore a doublet over their shirt, a ruff, an elegant jacket, and matching trunk hose, which were poofy pants that ended at the knee.

Oh no, this isn't for me!

I feel better in men's clothing!

Do you like my cloak?

COLLARS, RUFFS, AND CUFFS:
Often white, sometimes made of lace, they gave a touch of elegance to men's and women's clothing. Special iron supports were sometimes used to hold the rigid ruffs in place.

DOUBLET:
With or without sleeves, a doublet was a short coat worn by men over their shirt. Usually it was very richly decorated.

TRUNK HOSE:
Men of the time wore their pants short and puffed. They were often tight at the knee.

BODICE:
Rigid and tight, women would wear bodices under their clothing. A bodice could even come equipped with a frame that was used to keep the hooplike shape of women's skirts.

Oooooh . . . how elegant!

MEN'S SHOES:
These could be adorned with ribbons or be finely decorated.

to the men's fashion of the day *"Now that's more like it!"* she said.

When we were all dressed, we left the Tail Transporter. I **miniaturized** it and hung it around my neck.

We were in a humid, **DARK**, and **stinky** alley in London. It smelled like rotting wood and fish, so I guessed we were near the River Thames. **"Are you ready for a new adventure?"** Wild Willie cried enthusiastically.

"Huzzah! Yes, we're ready!" Benjamin, Maya, and Bugsy yelled together.

"No, I'm **not ready** in the slightest," I grumbled.

Just then, I realized there was a fifth squcak **MISSING**: Roborat-8's!

Where in the name of aged cheddar was he?

We looked long and hard for him, with no luck.

Maybe he had **dematerialized** for some strange robot reason, or maybe he went off by himself

to look for the professor. In any case, he had DISAPPEARED.

"Let's hope that tiny tin can is back by the time we're ready to leave. Otherwise, we'll be **imprisoned** in the past forever," I muttered uneasily. "Without him, the Tail Transporter won't work!"

We wandered through the alleys near the port, calling his name. Sometimes it seemed like I could hear his squeak from really far away, saying, "I'm here, Geronimoid!" But as much as I squinted and strained, I couldn't see him anywhere.

In the end, **RELUCTANTLY**, we were forced to abandon our efforts. We had to find a way to get into Elizabeth I's court, where Professor von Volt was probably waiting for us.

By now, it was evening, and we heard happy chatting and singing from a nearby tavern. We could also smell the delicious **scent** of cheese pie.

Mmmm . . . that delectable odor made me

realize how **hungry** I was. We decided to go in.

Inside, there was quite an **uproar**. All kinds of rodents filled the tables. Many were sailors who told of their adventures on the seven seas.

We sat in a corner to keep a low profile. The innkeeper brought us a pot of warm slop with stale cheese rinds floating in it, and we all dug in.

Despite my hunger, I couldn't help but notice the rodents sitting next to us. They were six gentlemice who were dressed very **elegantly**. One of them stood out because his eyes were piercing, his whiskers were long and dark, and his beard was **WELL TRIMMED**. He was asking his comrades a series of probing questions. "So, tell me: How many barrels of pepper do we have? How many chests full of silver? How many trunks of gold?"

One of them responded with a shaky squeak. "aLas, Sir Francis, we don't know! Our bookkeeper **DIED** this morning and he was the only one who knew how to read and count . . ."

Benjamin leaned in close. "Uncle G, I believe that is *Sir Francis Drake*, the famouse pirate!" he whispered in my ear.

A chill went down my tail. I gazed at Sir Francis and LISTENED intently.

"Scurvy sea cats! Are you saying we don't know how much **loot** we brought back from our battles at sea?"

Sir Francis Drake
*(Tavistock, England, 1540—
Panama, January 28, 1596)*
Sir Francis Drake was a notorious English sailor and pirate. From 1577 to 1580, he sailed around the globe, and when he returned, he was knighted by Queen Elizabeth I. He helped sabotage the Spanish Armada in 1587, which contributed to the legendary defeat of the Armada in 1588.

LONG LIVE
THE QUEEN!

Holey cheese, Benjamin was right! It was really the famouse Sir Francis Drake, and he seemed **madder** than a rat with a trap on his tail.

"You mean to tell me that we **don't know** how much booty we have for our Queen?" he exclaimed.

"Long live the Queen!" the others hastily declared.

All the other patrons jumped to their paws and declared, "Long live the Queen!"

I was so distracted thinking about the famouse pirate that I forgot to **JUMP** to my paws like the others. Sir Francis glared at me **suspiciously**.

"Mouse, tell me, why did you not pay tribute to the Queen like all the others? Are you perhaps an **enemy** of our beloved leader?" he demanded.

"Long live the Queen!" I cried quickly. And I took off my hat and bowed.

Once again everyone scrambled to their paws and called out, "Long live the Queen!"

When the room quieted down, Sir Francis turned to me again. "Why were you **STARING** at me? Were you eavesdropping, by chance? Are you a **spy**?" he thundered.

Wild Willie quickly intervened. "Oh no, you're mistaken, Sir Francis! My friend here is a **bookkeeper**, not a spy. He was staring at you because it seems you need one, and he would like to volunteer his services."

*Sovereigns were gold coins used in England during Elizabethan times.

Maya **pinched** my tail and murmured, "Tell them you're a bookkeeper, rookie! This is our chance to get close to you-know-who!"

I'm really not good with NUMBERS, but I had no choice. "It's t-t-true. I'm a b-b-bookkeeper!" I stammered.

Sir Francis removed a leather sack from his belt. It was full of **gold coins**. "Quit clucking, stranger! Are ten sovereigns* enough?"

I was taken off guard. "Oh! Er . . ." I muttered.

"So how about twenty, will that do?"

I opened my snout to answer, but before I could, Sir Francis squeaked again. "All right, I'll give you thirty, but that's my final offer!"

Long . . . live . . . the . . . Queen! Long live the Queen!

He threw thirty gold coins down in front of me.
Wild Willie quickly covered the coins with his
paw. "That will do, Sir Francis, that will do!"

Sir Francis looked us over from tail to toe. "All
right, you're **HiReD**! What's your name?"

"I am Geronymus van Stilton, and they are Wild
William, Lord Mayus, Benjamin, and Bugsy," I
replied.

"Very good. You have all night to inventory
everything loaded on my boat, the *Golden
Hind*.* Tomorrow we will be received by our
beloved queen," Sir Francis said, bowing.
Everyone repeated in unison, "Long live the Queen!"

Bugsy rolled her eyes. "This is more boring than

Hind is a word for a female deer, also called a doe.

Long . . . live . . . the . . . Queen! Long live the Queen! Huff!

a cheese-free sandwich! I can't handle all this **bowing** and scraping left and right!"

"You're right," Benjamin said. "It's better never to say the word *quee* —"

Bugsy covered his snout with her paw, but alas, it was too late! Once more, everyone shouted, "Long live the Queen!"

But there was at least one other rodent in the tavern who agreed with Bugsy. "That's enough! If another one of you utters *that name*, I will throw you in the **river**!" he blurted.

No sooner had he squeaked than a violent **FIGHT** broke out. We got out of there as fast as our paws could carry us.

We followed Sir Francis through the dark alleys near the port. Finally, we arrived at the pier where he'd docked his **GALLEON**, the legendary *Golden Hind*!

We scurried across a slippery, wobbly gangway as the dark waters of the port sparkled in the moonlight. I looked down and immediately felt dizzy. Then I slipped on a grease **spot**, flapping my paws like crazy to keep my **balance**.

Just when I was about to tumble into the **cold**, dark waters of the Thames, Wild Willie grabbed me by the tail.

"Watch your step, rookie!" he cried as I dangled over the water.

Maya giggled, and I turned **purple** with embarrassment. Holey cheese, I was making one

bad impression after the next!

Wild Willie got me back on my paws, and I tried to pull myself together.

Sir Francis Drake was waiting for me impatiently, tapping his paws on the railing of the deck. "Bookkeep, hurry, time's wasting away!"

Something told me that he was a mouse who was naturally GROUCHIER than a groundhog.

We followed him onto the deck, and he led us to a hatch that he opened with a key.

With a shiver, I thought about the goods I was about to take stock of. They were the booty of a terrifying PIRATE who'd sailed the seven seas and carried out countless raids, attacked innocent merchants, and even sank ships! It was a big job for a scaredy-mouse like me!

My paws began to tremble so much that I could barely keep my grip on the *feather*

pen Sir Francis had pawed me.

"So, are you ready, squidsnout?" he demanded.

I grabbed a long, rolled-up **scroll** and stammered, "Y-yes!"

He began to dictate the inventory. As Wild Willie held the scroll, I scribbled down the items Sir Francis listed, dipping the pen into the inkwell that Bugsy was holding for me. Benjamin blew on the paper so the ink would dry faster.

The list of goods included . . .

- 35 sacks of **black pepper** from Madagascar
- 80 pounds of dried sultana grapes
- 10 pots of **honey** from the Molucca Islands
- 42 sacks of jasmine tea from the Indies
- 12 sacks of **cacao** pods
- 8 cages with parrots
- 1 cage with a monkey
- 15 baskets of cayenne pepper
- 89 barrels of CINNAMON powder
- 15 jars of French **mustard**
- 30 bales of Chinese silk
- 8 rolls of the finest **lace** from Flanders

Sir Francis went on and on for hours. Finally, the light of DAWN cast thousands of silvery reflections on the waters of the Thames.

So much booty!

ARE YOU READY, BARNACLE BRAIN?

I was almost at the end of the superlong scroll. I had **CRAMPS** in my paws from writing so much. And then, finally, Sir Francis stopped.

He opened another chest, and I saw priceless **jewels** sparkle inside it: gold, silver, pearls, precious stones.

The pirate gazed at those marvels for a moment. "Are you ready, **BARNACLE BRAIN**? These are the last items we need to take stock of. And they are the most precious: They will go to enrich our **beloved queen's** treasure!"

"**Long live the Queen!**" we cried quickly, before he could get angry.

According to the custom of the time, I bowed and put my paw over my heart. Unfortunately, I moved my paw too hastily and accidentally stuck the feather pen in my **EYE**! Yee-ouch!

I yelled and accidentally stepped back on Wild Willie's **TAIL**. He stepped back and knocked against the bottle of ink, and it **SPRAYED** all over my whiskers!

To avoid the splatter, Benjamin jumped back and **STEPPED** on my paw. To dodge Benjamin, Bugsy stepped on my other paw, and Maya jumped on my tail!

Holey cheese, I was in agony!

"Stop that madness, you crab cake!" Sir Francis yelled. "You are the most **bungling** bookkeeper I've ever seen! I will take the damages out of your pay, you can be sure! Now clean yourself up so we don't make a bad impression. Scurry up or I'll **SLICE** off your tail!"

I quickly ran to the pirates' quarters to fix myself up. In the meantime, I rolled up the **superlong** scroll and stuck it in my pocket.

Then I looked at myself in the mirror to make sure I was presentable enough for the court. I didn't look half bad in those clothes! Who knows, maybe Maya would be **impressed** after all . . .

"Hurry up, fishface!" Sir Francis boomed. "You don't want the Que — I mean, **she** whom it's best not to name or we'll all have to start praising her all over again . . . you don't want *her* to **GET MAD**, do you?"

He was making me more **nervous** than a mouse in a lion's den. I scampered up to the top deck. Sir Francis and my friends were already there, waiting impatiently.

We all crossed the shaky gangway, and once more, I got dizzy and began to wobble. Once more, I tried to keep my balance by flapping my paws. Once more, I **SLIPPED** on the grease spot. And once more, Wild Willie tried to grab me by the tail!

Unfortunately, he didn't manage to catch me this time, and I ended up going into the river snoutfirst. I was **SOAKED** to the fur!

Maya and Wild Willie had to pull me out with a hook. Sir Francis stood watching impatiently. "Hurry, the Queen is waiting!"

Spitting out water, I hurriedly cried, "Long live the Queen!"

"Long live the Queen!" my friends echoed.

As soon as I reached **dry** land, Sir Francis began scolding me. "You're the peskiest bookkeep I've ever known! What, do you have seawater up your snout? Come on, climb onto this horse. **She** will be waiting for us in exactly half an hour at the Tower. And it's best not to keep her waiting! She's always in a bad mood there because of all the **BAD MEMORIES** . . ."*

"Huh? I don't understand . . . Why does she have bad memories of the Tower?" I asked.

Sir Francis didn't answer. He had already *galloped* off! And we followed him, crossing through the city of London . . .

*In 1554, Elizabeth's half sister, Mary, who was queen at the time, accused her of treason and locked her in the Tower of London for two months.

London

LONDON IN THE LATE 1500S

RIVER THAMES

Toward the end of the 1500s, London was developed mostly north of the River Thames. It was a city of narrow, winding, dark, and dirty roads. Many of the buildings were tenements that were up to six stories tall, with a workshop or a warehouse on the first floor, a dining room and a living room on the second floor, and other rooms on the upper floors. The buildings were often quite crowded, and poorer people lived squished together in just a few rooms.

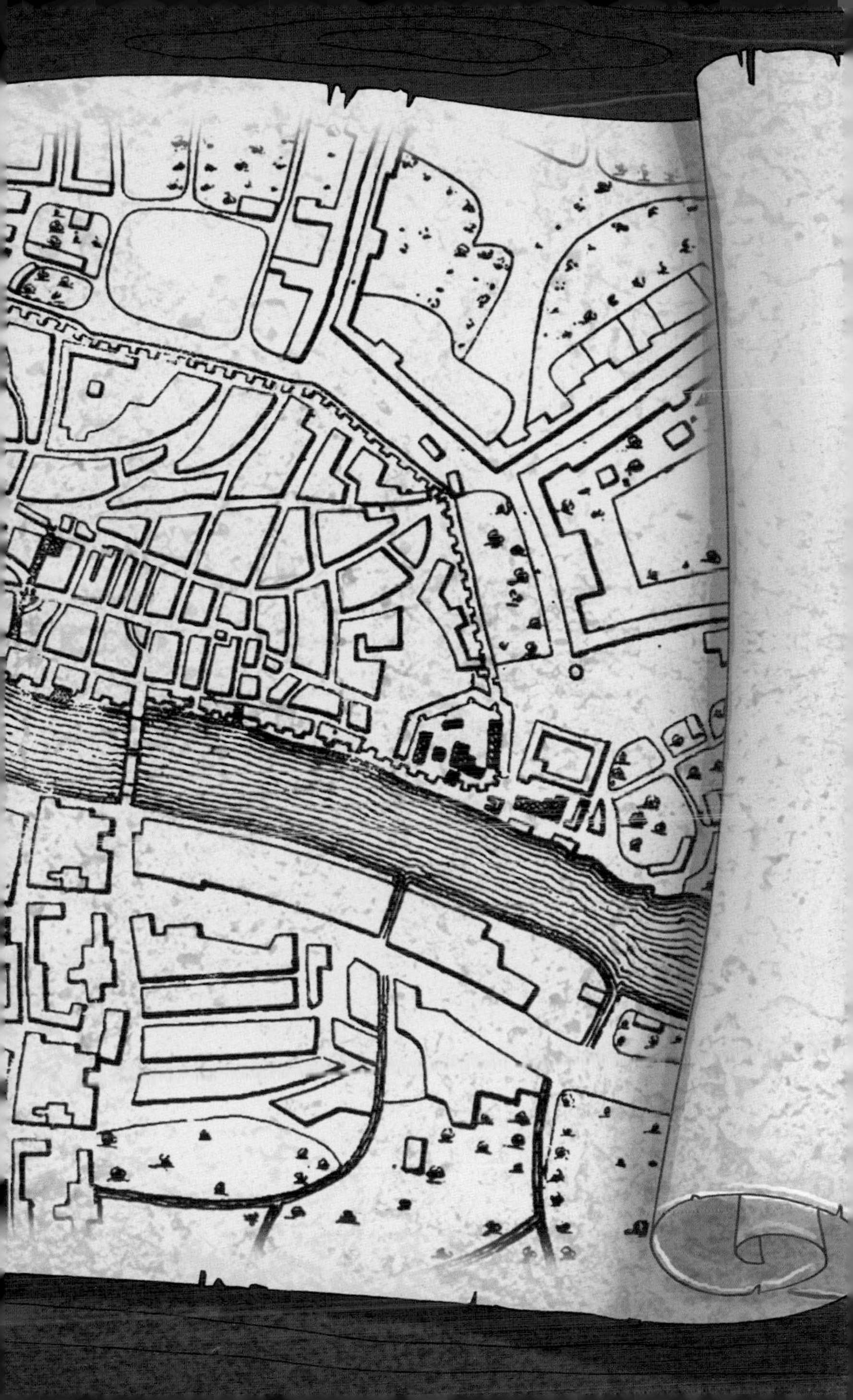

PLOP!
PLOP! PLOP!
PLOP! PLOP! PLOP!

As we galloped through the city, I looked around. The streets were **narrow**, dark, and dirty. The buildings were all different heights, and, from the shouting that echoed from various windows, you could tell that many, many rodents lived in them!

A female rodent dumped a bedpan out of a window and almost hit my snout.

Yuck, what a sour stench!

Oh, how I missed Roborat-8! He would have warned us to be careful. He would have **FILLED** my mind with information about the city, the manners of the court, and the TOWER OF LONDON!

"Poor Roborat-8. Who knows where or when he ended up?" I murmured.

For a moment, I thought I heard his voice whisper, "I'm right here, Geronimoid!" But it was probably just my overactive imagination.

Luckily, Bugsy was an ace at history, and she began to whisper to me. "Uncle G! The TOWER OF LONDON is the most ancient royal palace in London, but it was — I mean, it *is* — also used as a PRISON. When she was younger, Elizabeth I was accused of plotting against her half sister, Mary, who was Queen at the time, and she was locked up there!"

That **worried** me. "Sir Francis, why does the Quee — *she* — want to meet us at the Tower?"

"Well, if she's not happy with our gifts, she could have our snouts cut off!" Sir Francis responded.

"Wh-wha? Have our snouts cut off?" I cried.

"Yes, fishface, something small could displease her and . . . **thwack**! So try to behave yourself," he replied.

"Perhaps she went to check on the **ROYAL RAVENS**," one of the sailors added. "I'm sure you must know that she cares a lot about ravens, because of the **LEGEND**."

"What legend?" Benjamin asked.

"You must come from very far off not to know it, strangers!" the sailor replied. "According to the legend, as long as six ravens live in the Tower, the Crown and England will live on. But if the ravens should fly away, the Kingdom of England **_will fall_**!"

We had reached the Tower at last. As we approached, the six Royal Ravens bombarded me with some, er, royal **SOUVENIRS**! Yuck!

PLOP! PLOP! PLOP! PLOP! PLOP! PLOP!

Before I could protest, two guards dressed in uniforms bearing the crest of the Tudors — Queen Elizabeth's family — stepped forward. As

soon as they saw us, they lowered their lances.

"The Royal Ravens have shown a great fondness for you, sir," the first one greeted me. "You should be **HONORED**! But tell us, who are you and where are you going?"

Before I could respond, Drake declared, "He is my **bookkeeper**. And I am the *noble* Sir Francis Drake. And *she* is waiting for us!"

The guards stood at attention and let us pass. But as we did, I could hear them muttering, "*She*

is very **on edge** today! I wonder if these rodents will make it out of the Tower alive . . ."

I was about to turn around, but Wild Willie grabbed me. "Remember, rookie, we need to **LOOK FOR** Professor von Volt!" he whispered.

I gathered up my courage. I wanted to save my friend, and I also didn't want to look like a 'fraidy mouse in front of Maya again!

We walked through winding stone hallways. There were crowds of pages, couriers, ELEGANT

DAMES, and gentlemice with feathered hats and swishy capes. Everyone around us was whispering and *gossiping*.

"I wonder if Sir Francis has much **LONGER** to live . . ." one of the courtiers muttered.

A chamberlain trotted toward us. "Oh, Sir Francis! What a pleasure to see you still alive after your long voyage . . ."

Sir Francis grumbled at him, "What kind of **mood** is *she* in today?"

The other rodent raised his eyes to the sky. "Alas, this morning she is particularly *edgy* — she discovered someone rummaging through the crown jewels! Maybe you can calm her down with the list of **GOODS** you acquired for her on the seven seas!"

Sir Francis turned to me. "Did you hear that, cheesebrain? Be ready with the list!"

I reached my paw toward my **pocket** where I

had left the scroll for safekeeping. "Stay calm, Sir Francis, I have everything right here!" I replied.

But then I turned paler than a slice of Swiss, because when I put my paw in my pocket, I realized it was full of water. **GULP!**

My fear turned into terror when I felt a claw sink into my fur. There was a CRAB attached to my paw! Ouchie! But I didn't dare cry out, for we had reached the door to the throne room.

As we proceeded into the enormouse room, my heart was beating faster than the mouse who ran up the clock. I was overwhelmed with FEAR and **foreboding**. I could only imagine the state of the scroll with the list of Sir Francis's goods!

She was seated at the end of the room on a

gilded wooden throne. It was really her — Her Majesty Queen Elizabeth! (Long live the Queen!)

She stared at us with icy eyes. "Oh, Sir Francis! What have you brought for me this time? And who is this with you?"

Sir Francis bowed deeply. "Your Majesty, I have great **riches** for you! Now Geronymus, my bookkeeper, will read you the **precise**, accurate, and detailed record of everything that is held in the cargo hold of my galleon!"

He turned to me. "Go on, read it!" he hissed.

The courtiers stared at me . . .

Sir Francis Drake and his crew stared at me . . .

The Queen stared at me . . .

In that terrible silence, full of expectation, I solemnly took the scroll out of my pocket. It DRIPPED water and ink onto the floor.

Drip! Drip! Drip!

Drip!
Drip!
Drip!

YOUR BEAUTY HAS DAZZLED ME . . .

I unrolled the scroll with trembling paws, but, alas, the water had *smeared* all the ink!

The Queen was impatiently tapping her paws. "So? Are you going to read it or not?"

My brain was **boiling**. Frantically, I tried to figure out what to do. Suddenly, inspiration struck.

I threw myself on my knees and **DECLARED**, "I am so sorry, Your Majesty, I cannot read you anything because . . .

"Your beauty has dazzled me,
You've stunned me with your charm.
Your eyes have enchanted me,
Your fair fur does disarm!
You've captivated me with your grace,
Charmed me with your elegance,
You've declawed me with your dignity,
Bewitched me with your intelligence!"

Sir Francis shot me a **MENACING** look.

All the courtiers looked at me, STUNNED.

But I had eyes only for *her*, Queen Elizabeth, who was studying me closely.

After a moment of silence that seemed to stretch on forever, she broke into **laughter**. "Well done, rat! This poem in my honor is quite nice. It reminds me of the style of my beloved William Shakespeare!"

Sir Francis had been pulling out his sword to slice off my tail, but luckily, these words from the Queen stopped him short.

You've stunned me with your charm . . .

What?!

"I LiKE you. I'll take you on," she continued. "Tell me, rat, what you would like to do? Would you like to be the guardian of my Royal Ravens? I see by their tokens on your coat that they have already taken a liking to you. Or perhaps you would prefer to *write* the Royal Story of my Royal Life?"

I was quiet, UNCERTAIN what to do next.

Could I endure the ravens? I would constantly risk being bombarded by their . . . souvenirs. On the other paw, how long would I **Survive** if I were constantly following the Queen around? I could tell her mood was as **fickle** as the weather in England! She could lock me up in the Tower of London for the slightest mistake. *Rotten rats' teeth, what a horrifying thought!*

Wild Willie and Maya took advantage of my

hesitation. "Geronymus would be happy to write your Royal Biography!" Maya cried.

"Long live the Queen!" everyone shouted.

I bowed low. As I did, I muttered, "How do I always end up with these thankless jobs?!"

Maya shushed me. "Just be quiet and write, Stilton. And don't worry, if she decides to have your snout cut off, we'll come save you!"

"Be quiet and write, rookie!" Wild Willie added. "It's pretty much the only thing you're good at anyway . . ."

"Be **BRAVE**, Uncle G. You can do it!" Benjamin whispered encouragingly.

I sighed. I was scared, but I knew my friends were right. If I stayed close to the Queen, I'd have plenty of chances to find CLEOPATRA'S MIRROR.

So I bowed. "I would be honored to write the story of your life, Your Majesty."

She **smiled**, pleased. "Very well. Now Sir Francis, you can go get me more **RICHeS**. As for the report, don't worry about it this time. I forgive you! However, to make up for your negligence, I will take Geronymus and his friends in my service. The two young ones will be pages; the two gentlemice will be **TOWER GUARDS**!"

Sir Francis bowed and strode off.

So that is how I began to **follow** the Queen around all day, from dawn until midnight, when she would retreat to her quarters.

She dictated her memories to me **nonstop**. I *always* had to be at her side!

AT THE THEATER
WITH THE QUEEN

As time passed, the Queen began telling me more than the official version of events. Sometimes she would entrust me with her s̶e̶c̶r̶e̶t̶s̶ — some of which I would have preferred not to know. Being the Queen's confidant can be **DANGEROUS**!

Elizabeth was very happy with my service. One day, she told me, "Geronymus, tonight we're going to the **tHeater**! Shakespeare is putting on **A MIDSUMMER NIGHT'S DREAM**! You absolutely must write in my biography that I have always loved art, dance, and the theater. In addition to her many royal duties, a queen also has the right to **enjoy herself**!"

William Shakespeare

"Your Majesty, it would be a great honor to accompany you. I love the theater, too, especially the works of Shakespeare. And *A Midsummer Night's Dream* is my favorite. I know entire passages by heart!"

The Queen interrupted me, and I knew right away that I had blundered. You see, 1595 was the year Shakespeare WROTE *A Midsummer Night's Dream*, so there was no way I could've known it! Oh, I'd really put my paw in it this time . . .

"Tonight is the premiere of this comedy! How can you know it? Are you perhaps a soothsayer? Or are you such a good friend of Shakespeare that he let you read his works BEFORE they are performed?" she inquired.

I bowed until my whiskers grazed the ground. "Excuse me, Your Majesty, I cannot tell you everything: Even a humble scribe has his secrets."

Luckily, the Queen was in a good mood. She

burst out laughing. "Oh, that's true! Yes, you have the right to a few **secrets**, too."

So, chatting pleasantly, we scurried off to the theater. We took our seats in the part of the balcony reserved for the Queen. Maya, Wild Willie, Benjamin, and Bugsy were all there waiting for us.

The room was full, but strangely, the play was delayed. After a while, the crowd began to GRUMBLE and **rumble**.

The Queen leaned over and whispered in my ear impatiently. "Geronymus, go backstage and see what's happening. This waiting is getting on my nerves!"

I quickly obeyed. I'd learned it's better never to contradict a queen!

When I reached backstage, Shakespeare greeted me with agitation. "Ah, finally, you've arrived! I've been waiting for a substitute for my lead actor

Plonk!

for hours. Quick, get onstage — the audience is growing restless!"

Before I could protest, he slipped a fake donkey mask over my head and pushed me **ONSTAGE**. I couldn't see where to put my paws, so I TRIPPED and fell flat on my snout.

I let out a long, choked cry of pain, and everyone mistook it for a donkey's bray. The audience exploded with LAUGHTER, thinking it was part of the play!

I knew from the donkey head who my character

was. I had to play Nick Bottom, a weaver whom the mischievous **fairy** Puck turns into a donkey.

I also remembered that the queen of the fairies, Titania, would drink a **love** potion and fall in love with me!

I kept tripping because of the donkey head, but the performance was a **MOUSERIFIC** success anyway. At the end of the show, everyone leaped to their paws and applauded, even the Queen!

A Midsummer ∽ Night's Dream ∽

This famous comedy tells the story of two pairs of young lovers — Lysander and Hermia, and Demetrius and Helena. On a summer's night, there are many misunderstandings and lots of magical interference. Nonetheless, the couples declare their love. The mischievous fairy Puck, one of the most beloved of Shakespeare's characters, is the one who keeps the story moving.

WHAT A SURPRISE!

When we returned to the palace after the show, Queen Elizabeth was still raving about my performance. "Geronymus, I must give you a little gift. Follow me . . ."

She approached her desk and pressed a secret BUTTON. From the false bottom of a drawer, she took out a large iron key. Then she led me to her library, pressed the spine of a book, and suddenly the entire bookshelf turned in on itself, revealing a SECRET PASSAGE!

We scurried down a narrow spiral staircase until we found ourselves in front of a tiny red door. Elizabeth stuck the heavy iron key into the lock and, with a creak, the door opened.

The small room that lay before us was filled

with priceless JEWELS! It was Elizabeth's secret treasure!

There were enormouse mounds of golden coins and a large leather treasure chest finished with shiny brass. It was brimming with pearls of various **hues**: white, pink, yellow, gray, and even black.

On a shelf, there were seven ornate gold goblets. Each one contained **precious** stones: rubies, emeralds, sapphires, topaz, diamonds, aquamarine, and lapis lazuli. Three baskets of golden **filigree** held precious amber, turquoise, and coral pieces.

Her Majesty opened an engraved armoire. Inside there were precious garments, plus crowns and **tiaras** of every shape and size.

Elizabeth chose the largest **crown** and put it on. "This is my favorite! It's a shame that it makes my snout look so **BIG** . . ."

Then she picked up something from a shelf. I stared at it in wonder: It was CLEOPATRA'S MIRROR!

She admired herself, then turned toward me. Does your queen seem *regal* enough?"

I bowed until my whiskers grazed the ground. "Long live the Queen!"

From behind a heap of gold, I heard someone echo my words: "Long live the Queen!"

I was so surprised I nearly jumped out of my fur. "Who was that?"

"Oh, that? It's some scoundrel who wanted to rummage through my jewels," the Queen grumbled. "As punishment, I imprisoned him here, and I make him **polish** my money, piece by piece."

I looked in the direction the **squeak** had come from. There, I saw a mouse hunched over many shining coins. It was Professor von Volt! "Geronimo, thank goodmouse you've arrived!"

he whispered. "Did you read my message on the mirror? I wrote it when all seemed lost: The Queen had shut me in here, and the Paw Pro Portal was **damaged** during landing. I was afraid I'd never get home again!"

"My dear friend, I am so happy to see you!" I said to him. "I was at the Egyptian Mouseum in New Mouse City when I read your first message, but I also found the hieroglyphics you left for me in ancient Egypt. I've followed you here through half of history! Now let's **keep calm and scurry on**. In no time, we'll get you home to Mouse Island, back in the present day!"

At that moment, Elizabeth beckoned me. "Geronymus, dear mouse, come!"

"Quick, quick, go," the professor urged me.

I returned to the Queen. "Tell me, what would you like as a gift for your services?" she asked. "**Gold coins?** A medallion with my portrait on it? Or would you prefer a title? 'Sir Geronymus' has a nice ring to it!"

Once again, I **bowed** deeply. "Your Majesty, I ask you . . . for the release of that unlucky mouse who is here shining your money!"

My request enraged the Queen. "How dare you **DISMISS** my gifts?"

I tried to explain courteously. "Oh no, I'm not dismissing them! You've got the **WRONG** end of the cheese stick, Your Highness. You yourself suggested I pick the gift I preferred —"

But she was more **FURIOUS** than a fly stuck in fondue. "At least explain to me why you are making this **strange** request!" she demanded.

I smiled at my friend Professor von Volt. "Because, Your Majesty, friendship is the most precious gift!"

"So you are friends with this scoundrel?! I don't want you to write my biography anymore! I will have you both **thrown** into the Tower of London!" she cried.

At that moment, we heard squeaking. It was my friends! They had managed to **follow** me.

The minute Maya spotted Professor von Volt, a **SMILE** spread across her snout. "Geronimo, you found the professor! Now we can go home!"

The Queen lost it. "You are friends with that scoundrel, too? **Treason!**" she shrieked. Then she scurried off to find some guards.

Treason!!!

"Quick, we need to ESCAPE before the guards get here!" Wild Willie cried.

"But is this **ROOM** big enough to hold the Tail Transporter?" Maya asked.

Professor von Volt did some quick calculations. "Yes, it will fit! Quick, Geronimo, enlarge it . . ."

As soon as the Tail Transporter returned to its regular size, we scrambled inside, and . . . SURPRISE! We found Roborat-8!

"It's about time! It's been days that you've kept me imprisoned and MINIATURIZED in the Tail Transporter," he scolded us.

"We're sorry, Roborat-8! We **LOOKED** for you everywhere," I cried. "Now get the Rat-o-Ray ready. We need to go back home!" Roborat-8 got to work, and in a moment, we felt the usual **itchiness** all over our fur. This time, I didn't complain, because I knew we would rematerialize in New Mouse City!

FINALLY HOME!

After another minute, we had all **rematerialized** in Professor von Volt's laboratory, dressed in our usual clothes. We felt completely **scrambled**, but happy to be home again.

Being back in New Mouse City was **sweeter** than cheese dumplings with syrup on top!

Dewey hugged the professor. A single **TEAR** of happiness left a track down the fur on his snout.

Dewey!

Uncle Paws!

"Uncle Paws, finally! I was afraid I would **NEVER** see you again!" he cried.

Professor Von Volt smiled. "Dear Dewey, I thought I would never be able to get home again! It's only thanks to Geronimo that I am SAVED!"

I blushed. "Oh, please don't thank me. I didn't do anything special. I could never have done it without the help of my dear **FRIENDS** Wild Willie, Maya, Benjamin, Bugsy, and Roborat-8!"

Roborat-8 jumped down from the Tail Transporter, crying, "Dewey, I missed you!"

I missed you!

Dewey hugged him tenderly. "I missed you, too, little robot!"

Professor Von Volt turned to us. "Roborat-8 isn't just my most successful invention, he is almost like a son to me! He can feel real

feelings, and he keeps Dewey and me company."

I smiled. "It's true, he has a **generous** heart! He just has one defect . . . he never stops chattering! By the way . . . how do you turn him **off**? I couldn't find the switch . . ."

"What about you, Geronimoid?! You aren't exactly **defect-free**," Roborat-8 replied. "You are a 'fraidy mouse, a clumsypaws, and a total cheesebrain. Why, you accidentally left me

miniaturized inside the Tail Transporter! You suffer from seasickness, and, most of all, you are a complete cheddarface! But I love you anyway!"

Then he grabbed me by the paw and dragged me into a wild celebratory dance through the lab. "COME ON, LET'S CELEBRATE! CELEBRAAAAAAATE!"

Professor von Volt burst out laughing. "Roborat-8 doesn't have an OFF switch, he has a voice command. To turn him off, you just have to tell him, 'Go to bed, Roborat-8!'"

As soon as the professor uttered those words, Roborat-8 switched off. He immediately began to snore loudly. ZZZZZZ!

When he dropped my paw, I tumbled to the floor. For the first time since our journey had begun, I realized how WEARY I was.

I felt like I had lived for two thousand years!

I felt like my bones were broken, my **paws** were in pieces, my knees were wobbly, my whiskers were droopy, and my tail was limp . . .

I turned to my friends. They, too, **LOOKED** like they were about to fall asleep where they stood!

"Professor, friends, you're all exhausted. Please go **REST**! I'll head to the mouseum to see Cyril B. Sandsnout and tell him that the **hidden message** from Caesar is still inside the mirror's handle."

Maya scurried over and stared at me with

Ummm, th-thanks . . .

Geronimo, you're awesome!

her marvemouse brown eyes. "Good for you, Geronimo! You really brought your A game! You may not bc **courageous**, but you conquered your **FEARS** and you did everything you could to help your friends. You thought of others before yourself!"

I was so **overcome** with feeling that I nearly tripped over my own tail. "But now is not the time to collapse, rookie." She **giggled**. "We need to go see Professor Sandsnout. I'm hcre with you all the way to the end!"

"You said it, Cuz! I wouldn't miss the end of this **adventure** for anything in the world," Wild Willie added.

"We want to come with you, too," Benjamin and Bugsy said together.

I was moved by their devotion. I wiped a tear from my snout. What a terrific team we had turned into!

WHAT DAY IS IT?

Just when everything was getting back to normal again, I felt a sudden PANG of anxiety. "Dewey, what day is it?"

"It's **Wednesday**. Why?" Dewey replied.

"Oh no! Professor Sandsnout's conference has already begun!" I cried. "If we don't get there in time, we won't be able to **prove** the mirror's authenticity, and he could lose his job!"

We **DARTED** over to the mouseum, but when we arrived, it was too late! There was a crowd streaming out of the room.

A very **disheartened** Professor Sandsnout was alone in the middle of the conference room. He was staring at Cleopatra's mirror on the table in front of him.

I grabbed the **mirror** and jumped onto

the table. "Wait! Don't go! We have **proof** that Cleopatra's mirror is authentic!" I cried.

A rodent stopped and turned around, curious.

"Isn't that *Geronimo Stilton*?" he hissed. He sounded scandalized.

"Yes it's me — Stilton, Geronimo Stilton!" I said. "And I am here to prove the authenticity of Cleopatra's mirror and **DEFEND** the honor of a serious scholar, Professor Cyril B. Sandsnout!"

The mirror is authentic!

"That other one there with the big whiskers and the explorer's hat, isn't that Wild Willie, the famouse treasure hunter?" another rodent asked.

"Yes, it's me! And I am here for the same reason," Wild Willie thundered.

"We are here to HELP the professor, too," Maya, Benjamin, and Bugsy exclaimed.

The room had filled up again. The crowd was WHISPERING, commenting, "Okay, let's hear these crazy mice out . . ."

"All right, but this better be good," one mouse cried.

I felt my whiskers shaking from the stress. You see, I don't like public squeaking. I am a mouse who is very, very shy.

Benjamin took me by the paw "Be brave, Uncle G!" he whispered.

"Come on, Uncle G!" Bugsy winked at me.

Maya gave me a pat on the tail, and Wild Willie

gave me a slap on the shoulder. "Come on, let 'em have it, rookie!"

I was about to begin squeaking when a rodent with an **arrogant** air stepped forward. "Hurry up! Don't waste my time. I have a lot to do, because tomorrow I will become the `new director` of the Egyptian Mouseum!"

It was Martin McSnootersnout, Cyril B. Sandsnout's rival!

Quickly, I unscrewed the handle of Cleopatra's mirror and pulled out Caesar's note. "I will be brief. Here is the proof of the mirror's authenticity. It is a **message** written by Caesar to Cleopatra, and it has always been here, **hidden** in this mirror's handle!"

The scholars **OPENED**

their eyes wide in amazement. "Ooooh! This is unbelievable! Amazing!"

A dignified-looking scholar EXAMINED the message for a moment. "There's no doubt: This proves that the mirror truly belonged to Cleopatra!" she announced.

His ears drooping in embarrassment, Professor McSnootersnout slipped out of the room.

Professor Sandsnout would get to stay in his position as director of the mouseum! I breathed a sigh of RELIEF. Our mission had ended in the best possible way. I was so happy!

But I was also a bit sad. Soon the calmness of everyday life would return, and I had to admit that I'd miss the adventures I'd had with my FRIENDS Roborat-8, Wild Willie, and especially Maya!

Ah, what a fascinating rodent!

Just then, Maya scampered over to me. "I am

proud of you, rookie!" Then she **kissed** me on the tip of my whiskers.

I was about to faint, but she grabbed my paw, laughing, "Don't faint now, rookie, we need to **celebrate**!"

Okay, dear reader, I have to admit it. I had a huge **CRUSH** on her!

But this is another story, and perhaps I will tell it to you another time . . . or my name isn't Stilton, *Geronimo Stilton*!

Don't miss my first three journeys through time!

THE JOURNEY THROUGH TIME

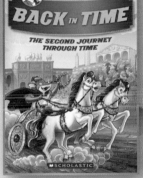

BACK IN TIME:
THE SECOND JOURNEY THROUGH TIME

THE RACE AGAINST TIME:
THE THIRD JOURNEY THROUGH TIME

Be sure to read all my fabumouse adventures!

#1 Lost Treasure of the Emerald Eye

#2 The Curse of the Cheese Pyramid

#3 Cat and Mouse in a Haunted House

#4 I'm Too Fond of My Fur!

#5 Four Mice Deep in the Jungle

#6 Paws Off, Cheddarface!

#7 Red Pizzas for a Blue Count

#8 Attack of the Bandit Cats

#9 A Fabumouse Vacation for Geronimo

#10 All Because of a Cup of Coffee

#11 It's Halloween, You 'Fraidy Mouse!

#12 Merry Christmas, Geronimo!

#13 The Phantom of the Subway

#14 The Temple of the Ruby of Fire

#15 The Mona Mousa Code

#16 A Cheese-Colored Camper

#17 Watch Your Whiskers, Stilton!

#18 Shipwreck on the Pirate Islands

#19 My Name Is Stilton, Geronimo Stilton

#20 Surf's Up, Geronimo!

#21 The Wild, Wild West

#22 The Secret of Cacklefur Castle

A Christmas Tale

#23 Valentine's Day Disaster

#24 Field Trip to Niagara Falls

#25 The Search for Sunken Treasure

#26 The Mummy with No Name

#27 The Christmas Toy Factory

#28 Wedding Crasher

#29 Down and Out Down Under

#30 The Mouse Island Marathon

#31 The Mysterious Cheese Thief

Christmas Catastrophe

#32 Valley of the Giant Skeletons

#33 Geronimo and the Gold Medal Mystery

#34 Geronimo Stilton, Secret Agent

#35 A Very Merry Christmas

#36 Geronimo's Valentine

#37 The Race Across America

#38 A Fabumouse School Adventure

#39 Singing Sensation

#40 The Karate Mouse

#41 Mighty Mount Kilimanjaro

#42 The Peculiar Pumpkin Thief

#43 I'm Not a Supermouse!

#44 The Giant Diamond Robbery

#45 Save the White Whale!

#46 The Haunted Castle

#47 Run for the Hills, Geronimo!

#48 The Mystery in Venice

#49 The Way of the Samurai

#50 This Hotel Is Haunted!

#51 The Enormouse Pearl Heist

#52 Mouse in Space!

#53 Rumble in the Jungle

#54 Get into Gear, Stilton!

#55 The Golden Statue Plot

#56 Flight of the Red Bandit

The Hunt for the Golden Book

#57 The Stinky Cheese Vacation

#58 The Super Chef Contest

#59 Welcome to Moldy Manor

The Hunt for the Curious Cheese

#60 The Treasure of Easter Island

#61 Mouse House Hunter

#62 Mouse Overboard!

The Hunt for the Secret Papyrus

#63 The Cheese Experiment

#64 Magical Mission

#65 Bollywood Burglary

The Hunt for the Hundredth Key

#66 Operation: Secret Recipe